PARIAH

A VASILY KORSOKOVACH MYSTERY

VASILY KORSOKOVACH INVESTIGATES
BOOK ONE

CHRISTOPHER H. JANSMANN

Ephram Cotte
& Company

ISBN-13: 978-1-7373523-0-3 (Kindle)
ISBN-13: 979-8-5114230-9-8 (Paperback)
ISBN-13: 978-1-7373523-1-0 (Library Bound)
ISBN-13: 978-1-960914-27-9 (Hardcover)

Cover design by: Chris Jansmann

Library of Congress Control Number: 2021911242

Printed in the United States of America

For Paula:

My love, my muse, my everything

Books by this Author

Chronological Order

Blindsided

Pariah

Outsider

Peril

Ditched

Bygones

Downhill

Duality

Focus

Bewitched

Requiem

Vengeance

Mirage

Solitude

Sean Colbeth Investigates

Blindsided

Outsider

Downhill

Duality

Bewitched

Vengeance

Solitude

Vasily Korsokovach Investigates

Pariah

Peril

Ditched

Bygones

Focus

Requiem

Mirage

Shorts

Snow Drifts

Contents

One 1
Two 6
Three 12
Four 22
Five 31
Six 39
Seven 47
Eight 54
Nine 60
Ten 64
Eleven 74
Twelve 80
Thirteen 85
Fourteen 90
Fifteen 95
Sixteen 101
Seventeen 106
Eighteen 111
Nineteen 117
Twenty 123
Twenty-One 129
Twenty-Two 137
Twenty-Three 142
Twenty-Four 147
Twenty-Five 154
Twenty-Six 158
Twenty-Seven 166
Twenty-Eight 174
Twenty-Nine 181
Epilogue 187

Afterword 191
Acknowledgements 193
About the Author 195

One

John Wayne International Airport – better known as the gateway to Orange County – was a small facility, especially when compared with its peers in California. Stacked up against Los Angeles International, there was no question it was a cozy destination, though to my mind it still dwarfed our rather aspirational Portland International Jetport. While it had cost me dearly to fly to John Wayne, it was offset by how much closer I would be to my new condo; it didn't hurt that my new Chief wouldn't have to go that far out of his way to drop me off. As I stepped out onto the Arrivals sidewalk, duffle in hand, I smiled a bit in anticipation of a new adventure – or several, given I had the contact information of the rather cute flight attendant who had coyly told me about his twelve-hour layover, subtly hinting he'd love some company later that evening.

Winter in Southern California alternated between modestly warm days and bouts of frigid, wet weather. The drizzle just beyond the covered sidewalk wasn't entirely unexpected, and I pulled the windbreaker a little tighter against the gusting breeze; compared to the subzero temperatures I'd just left, it felt positively tropical to me. Surfing looked to be out for the balance of the Thanksgiving holiday weekend, though, which suited me perfectly; I had to decide whether to go through with swinging by my parents to pick up my beach gear or simply replacing it all on my first trip to the beach. Given how we had left things fifteen years earlier, I suspected very little of my personal items remained; still, my mother despised throwing out *anything*, so there was a chance.

With the time difference from the East Coast, I'd arrived in the early evening; given the clouds, it was hard to tell how far below the horizon the sun had sunk at that hour, short of the gathering gloom beyond the bright streetlights. A part of me wondered if the lousy weather was a harbinger of things to come; not being overly superstitious – at least, outside of competitive swimming – I shrugged it off and scanned the traffic for my ride. The text from Chief Andrews had simply said he was circling; when a logoed SUV for the Rancho Linda Police Department pulled to the curb, I smiled and gave a half wave.

Tossing my gear in the backseat, I slid into the passenger side and shook hands with the grandfatherly head of my new department. "Detective Korsokovach," he greeted as he swiftly pulled back into the stream of traffic. "How was your flight?"

Thinking back to the Greek god who had made a point of doting on me, I smiled. "Not bad. We had a nice tailwind and few bumps."

"Good," he replied. "I *hate* flying. Gives me the creeps."

"Really?" I asked, eyes wide as I undid the ponytail I'd worn since Portland. Gathering it back up into a more casual half flip, I continued. "It's the fastest way to get anywhere."

"Maybe. I had a great uncle who worked for Southern Pacific during the golden age of passenger rail; I know Amtrak isn't quite the same, but I'll never be convinced that there isn't a finer way to travel than by train."

"I've never done it," I confessed.

"You should try it sometime. My wife loves how spacious the seats are; if it's more than a day's journey, we'll book a cabin and truly soak up the view from our private room."

"I'll keep that in mind."

"You're living in Anaheim?" he asked as he stepped on the enhanced accelerator police vehicles enjoyed and eased onto the freeway.

"Yeah," I said. "Despite the amazing package you offered me, I can't afford to live in Rancho Linda. And," I smiled a bit, "I'm a bit of a Disney fan."

I could see him roll his eyes. "Fireworks every night? Count me out."

I laughed. "My balcony should have a nice view of it, actually."

"Jesus," he said. "Well, better you than me."

Traffic was typical California, even for a holiday, and as he focused on avoiding getting into a collision, our conversation paused for a bit. Thinking about my parents had unleashed all of the usual emotions I had surrounding my family, none of them positive; watching the cars jockey for position distracted me enough to think a bit about the wider picture of returning to my home turf.

I had been the quintessential Southern California kid, growing up in a beach-front town two over from Anaheim. When I hadn't been in the pool, working my way toward a future spot on the U.S. Olympic team, I could be found riding the waves or soaking up the sun on the wide, sandy beaches that part of the state was known for. I was convinced my hair had lightened up due to endless hours of being exposed to the sun as I had; in my early teens, I'd taken to wearing the smallest suit possible at the pool to ensure my tan appeared to be full body at the beach, turning more than a few heads and generating those first dates where I began to explore my sexuality. Shaking my head, it occurred to me that my self-identity was closely bound to those formative years and wondered how much sooner I'd have come out had the right support been present within my own family.

My parents had been paragons of the community, and when they produced a star athlete, became something more. The pressure for them to have the perfect photogenic family had trickled down into an iron grip on my own life; I was expected to be in the pool, ever improving, or behind a desk, doing the same with my academics. Surfing had been the only permissible escape, given how it had "fit" the image of a child my parents had hoped would ultimately make his way into modelling or Hollywood. Thankfully, Coach Roberts had scouted me; though training as an Olympian had its own challenges, he managed to provide me with a valuable excuse to avoid the trite path my parents had planned for me.

The rhythmic slapping of the wipers against the windshield brought me back; Chief Andrews seemed to sense my return and cleared his throat. "I know you don't officially start until Monday, but I thought you might want to get into your first case." He paused and glanced at me. "Plus, it'll let me get your unmarked to you a bit faster."

"Sure," I said, intrigued. "What am I looking at?"

"The files are on your desk, including your laptop and the passwords for the network," he said as he shifted lanes. "Read over the materials this weekend and we'll chat first thing on Monday."

"Okay," I said, more intrigued that he'd not directly answered my question.

"Look," he continued, "I feel like I should level with you."

"Okay," I replied more slowly. "Am I getting fired already?"

"Nothing like that," he chuckled. "No, there are two things that you need to know before you start." He sped up a bit to slide around a car, swearing slightly. "Damn drivers. Yeah, uh, so first, I'm not the only one who looked you up on the web."

I nodded. "My life is pretty much there," I acknowledged. "Comes with being a Gold Medal winner."

"Yeah," he said, then glanced at me. "Rancho Linda is a pretty conservative community," he continued. "And some of the force – your colleagues – reflect that. To be honest, I'd hoped they would be a bit more open minded, given it's the fucking new millennium, but the scuttlebutt I am hearing is telling me otherwise."

"What are you trying to tell me?" I asked, a bit surprised at his language. It seemed odd coming from a man who looked a bit like everyone's favorite grandparent. Then I started to nod. "Ah. The article," I sighed, referencing what had been at the time a multiple-page interview I'd given to *The New York Times Magazine* the year I'd competed. Part of the article had dealt with my coming out experience, with a small section discussing the challenges of being a gay athlete. "Are you seriously saying I'm joining a homophobic department?"

"Fuck no," Andrews said, his continued salty language underscoring his concern. "But there are enough that you are likely to have a rough transition." He glanced at me again. "I hired you because your record speaks to being in the top tier of investigators in the country. Whatever else you are is your own business – and not relevant to how you do your job." Andrews sighed.

I felt my face heat up a bit. "As well it shouldn't."

"Exactly."

We rode along in silence for a bit, giving me a few moments to digest what he'd just told me. It was highly irregular for a head of department to be quite so candid, which told me something. I wasn't entirely sure what; smiling privately at my ghosted reflection in the passenger window, I realized Sean would have known. Much had I learned from my friend and mentor, yet that unusual gut instinct of his was not something I'd been able to replicate.

Someday.

I looked back at Chief Andrews. "What was the second thing?"

Andrews started to laugh. "I'm too old for this bullshit," he replied. "So, I'm retiring at the end of the year."

My eyes had to have widened in shock. "You're... leaving?" I asked.

"Yeah," he said as we turned and drove down an offramp. "Welcome to Rancho Linda, Detective."

Two

The SUV that I'd been assigned wasn't terribly different than the one I'd had back in Maine, other than being several model years newer. That alone didn't make it any easier to park in the svelte underground garage of my condo building; given my status as a new tenant, I'd had to drive to the lowest level before finding the space assigned to my townhome, and barely had enough space to open the driver's side door.

My leasing agent had included the keys and a security fob in the envelope that had my signed paperwork, paperwork I'd received just days before telling Sean I was leaving. Having not physically visited the building, I had to flip through the packet to figure out how to get my condo's location before using the fob to access the elevator. Given the extraordinary salary I'd been promised – many multiples more than my haul working for Sean – I'd splurged and signed a lease-to-own agreement for a top floor space angled toward Disneyland. It was four hundred extra a month, and though it remained to be seen if it was worth it, just the fact that I *could* splurge meant something to me.

Exiting on the seventh floor, the elevator lobby was just as tasteful as the building itself, with a small set of couches facing a tall window fronting Katella Avenue. At that late hour, standing slightly to the side I could make out lights from the massive sign for the Honda Center in the distance, and the tip of the Angels stadium. I wasn't really a fan of either hockey or basketball, but more than a few baseball players had graced teenage fantasies back in the day. I made a mental note to see if the Red Sox were coming to town next season before following the directional placards to find my new home at the end of the hallway.

Closing the door behind me, I tossed the files Andrews had provided to me onto the kitchen counter, dropped my duffel onto the tile then set the laptop backpack against the cabinet. Flipping on the lights revealed the high-end kitchen, complete with marble countertops and stainless-steel appliances. Sliding back down the short hallway from the door, I located the half-bath that also served as a laundry room, nodding at the empty spaces where said appliances would normally be and wondering if there were any Black Friday weekend deals I could still get in on.

The living/dining area was just in front of the kitchen, with floor-to-ceiling windows facing Disneyland in the distance. I unlocked the sliding glass door and stepped out onto the small patio, hearing the noise of the city as I leaned on the railing. I'd forgotten how *loud* California could be, for even at the height of tourist season, Route One never seemed more than a muted hiss. Looking out across the night, I smiled, for there in my direct line of sight was the illuminated peak of the Matterhorn. No question, I had landed a prime position for watching the nightly fireworks spectacular I had grown up loving.

My master bedroom was down a short hallway, its door opposite a small linen closet. It wasn't much, but it was all mine. And I loved every square foot of it. Of course, it would have been *better* with some furniture, but for now the thick pile of the carpet looked as though I'd be able to get by for a few nights.

Setting my iPhone on the counter, I could see it was nearly nine local time; my body said it was much later, but I still felt wired. Grabbing my overnight bag, I tested out the glass-walled shower of my new master bath, eyeing the unusual garden tub next to it. As much time as I spent in the pool, taking a bath held little appeal to me, but it was a nice touch, nonetheless.

After adding towels to my list of items I needed to purchase that weekend, I shook off as much water as I could before tossing on my sleeping pants and padding back out to the kitchen. Chief Andrews had left me curious as to the case I was to be the lead on, and it seemed prudent to dive in while I still had some stamina. Sean came to mind again as I pulled out the laptop and saw it was a MacBook. He'd long been part of the Cult of Steve Jobs, though not *quite* rabid enough to stand in line at the nearest Apple store when the latest iPhone became available. Flipping the lid open, I hunted down the credentials I'd been given and logged in before turning to the paper files and spreading them out along the breakfast bar.

Given we were in the modern era of police work, the folders weren't terribly thick and were comprised mostly of high-definition crime scene photos. I smiled slightly at that, for Sean had rarely printed photos himself, preferring to view them on his laptop or tablet so he could easily zoom in on details. Sliding the photos to the side, I wondered if this was to be a regular occurrence, seeing Sean in everyday actions little and big. I hoped not.

As concerns over cybersecurity had grown over the last few years, most police departments had tightened up how investigators were able to connect to the office remotely. It appeared Rancho Linda was no exception; while I was generally in favor of secure computing, I lost twenty minutes getting the virtual private networking software configured properly on the laptop. Finally able to connect to the VPN for the Rancho Linda department, I logged into their master database and punched up the case number from the sticky note Chief Andrews had provided. In moments I was looking at the virtual folder for the case, and started to scan through the summary. Written by the original investigating officer – one Mark Freidman, a detective of the same rank as myself who joined the department a year prior from a small town close to San Diego – the case seemed to be about a missing manuscript, apparently stolen from a local resident in the dead of night some weeks earlier. A nationally renowned historian, her latest work had been on a computer taken (among other things) during the robbery; somewhat tragically, the housekeeper had been killed by an unknown weapon. The author had been out of town and had returned to a smashed door and dead employee.

No leads had been generated in the murder, nor had the computer or other items stolen appeared in pawn shops in the greater Los Angeles area. Oddly, it wasn't the author that had reported the missing manuscript; no, it was the *publisher* who had brought it to the attention of the department, as it appeared there were no backups and there was an impending deadline for publication. Returning to the photos, I sorted through them to get to the body of the housekeeper. The coroner had taken a photo from behind, showing her face-down on an ornate oriental carpet. Squinting, it looked to me like she was wearing some form of uniform, something close to what I'd seen on *Downton Abbey*. That told me something about her employer and how she viewed herself in society; I'd grown up with plenty of people who felt their rarified air was never to be breathed by the "help."

A close up showed where the fatal blow to the skull had been; flipping back to the report on the computer, it had been inconclusive as to the weapon, though the ME had made a general call that it was roundish. Nothing remotely close to resembling the wound had been found in the house, though. Skipping down a few lines, I confirmed that the woman had been of Asian descent and in her late sixties, employed close to thirty years by the victim. No other hired help had been on that night, though there was apparently a chef and a gardener on the payroll. The latter had me pulling up the home on the department's GIS system, and my eyes bugged out to see it was the very definition of an estate.

Intrigued, I sifted through the records in the electronic file and found the property record from the assessor's office, which in turn had been linked to a brief writeup on the ownership history; the first few paragraphs, written by someone I assumed was an admin in the department, raised my eyebrows. Built by a former movie producer who had been big during the Golden Age of Hollywood, the estate had been an isolated outpost for fashionable society until the population had grown to surround it. Sitting on twenty acres on the edge of modern-day Rancho Linda, it had been carved out of an orange farm that, at the time, had been owned by the family of a future President of the United States. Once the studio system dissolved, the producer faded into obscurity and died alone in the mansion in nineteen-eighty; five years later, the author purchased it shortly after her second best-seller had been published. According to Google – and you can totally rely on the facts it presents, of course – it seemed that book was twelve books earlier; the fourteen published so far had covered a range of topics, from Presidents to the Spanish-American War to (of all things) baseball and Walt Disney. All were blockbusters, and book fifteen was rumored to be on the Westward Expansion based on the primary materials from Lewis and Clark.

Oddly, the book was years overdue.

That made me frown a bit, and I backed up again to the library website for the University of Eastern Maine. As an alum, I still had access to all of the research resources they provided and given the tiny budget Sean had been working with in Windeport, had come to rely on them when doing backgrounds on cases I worked. It took a few moments, but I located the catalog search function and quickly punched in the name from the file:

Frankenhoffer, Rosalia

The classic *please wait* flashing symbol appeared, and then a moment later her list of books appeared. Running my finger along the screen, I confirmed what Google had initially told me: there was generally a two-year gap between titles, which seemed to make sense given the amount of research the various subjects required. Her most recent book, *Walt Disney and His Animated View of the Future,* had been published eleven years ago; I wasn't a historian by any stretch, but a decade seemed like a long time to make a publisher wait. I shrugged, wondering if it had just been that much more difficult to go through the primary sources from the early nineteenth century.

As I considered the non-sequitur, my iPhone chimed a new text message. It made me groan, for no fewer than a dozen had come in from Sean, stretching back to the very hour I'd left him standing, slack-jawed, in the hallway at Maine Medical. The image of him in skintight black spandex from head to toe *did* make me smile, though, for I was quite certain he didn't know what sort of an effect seeing him that way had on me. Expecting to ignore yet another text from him, I was surprised to see it was instead from the flight attendant I'd met.

I groaned again, for I'd forgotten my quasi-promise to join him for drinks.

Carlos: *Dude, you've left me hanging all hot and bothered.*

Vas: *Sorry – got called in 2 work early. Still want to hook up?*

Carlos: *Are you f**ing kidding me? Get that cute ass of yours over here.*

I smiled as the dark-haired wonder provided the address of the hotel he was at. My eyebrows went up a bit at the photo he appended to express his enthusiasm. I was half tempted to beg off, but I couldn't deny the image he'd sent suddenly had me feeling a bit frisky. It certainly hadn't helped thinking of Sean in spandex.

Unsure of when, exactly, I might get back to the condo, I closed down everything, pulled on an old UEM Swimming t-shirt and rather optimistically stuffed a few condoms into my wallet from my overnight bag. I couldn't deny that my first hours in California had been anything but uneventful, and as I happily whistled down the hallway to the elevator, it felt like things were looking up finally.

Which, of course, they weren't.

Three

Carlos wasn't kidding about the length of time for his layover – twelve hours *on the dot* meant he had to report to John Wayne close to four that morning. We'd made the most of the time he'd had, though, and I was privately thankful he wasn't a pilot for he'd gotten very little rest. Leaning on my elbow, the sheet of the massive California King pulled to just above my waist, I watched as he slid his uniform pants over his impressively toned ass and tried not to coax him back for one final round. Turning, he pulled on his uniform top over a well-muscled torso, smiling at me slightly as he slowly did up the buttons before reaching for his coordinating tie.

"Where to today?" I asked casually, knowing there was no way the sheet was hiding how I was feeling at that moment.

"Nightmare day," he sighed. "Here to San Francisco, then Las Vegas, Tucson, Chicago and finally Boston. If we are on time, we'll turn Boston and get as far as Dallas before it's over."

I frowned. "When will you be back in California?"

Knotting his tie, he sat on the bed. "I won't," he said. "At least, not any time soon. I'm based in Dallas. I did this gig as a favor for someone who needed to swap."

"Oh," I said. "So that's that, then."

"Doesn't mean you can't come to Dallas," he smiled as he snaked his hand under the sheet.

I tried not to moan as he started to work me over. "I suppose..." I replied huskily. "I've only visited Texas long enough for the odd national swim meet back in the day."

"I know," he smiled wider. "I looked you up after you gave me your contact info."

My eyes had been half-closed but snapped open as I realized what had happened. "Ah," I said as I shifted to pull out from his grasp. "So that is what this is, then."

Carlos looked at me, his face flushing slightly. "No - I mean, not *entirely*," he said as his face flamed darker.

I waved at him and sighed. "You wouldn't be the first," I said as I rolled to the side of the bed and threw back the sheet, grabbing my shirt and sleeping pants from the floor. "I hope you enjoyed it."

"You're not actually *hurt*, are you?" Carlos asked incredulously from behind me as I slid my pants on. "My God. I mean, come on! What did you think was really going on here?"

Jamming my feet into my sneakers, I tugged my shirt over my head and then reached for my keys, phone and wallet. "Absolutely nothing," I said icily. "Have a pleasant flight," I added as I brushed past him and out the door of the suite.

The halls of the four-star hotel were brightly lit but empty; I sulked in silence as I rode the elevator to the underground parking garage. Carlos was the latest in a long line of one-night stands I'd had over the years that got off on spending the night with an Olympian. I invariably felt used in the worst conceivable way, and yet I seemed doomed to continually repeat the cycle. I was sure there was something there psychologically that begged to be looked into, but I truly didn't want to unlock that hidden part of me. Not yet.

As I slid into the SUV, my iPhone buzzed. Flipping it up I saw it was a text from Carlos; I deleted the message without reading it, blocked his number and dumped his contact information. It was a shit teenager move, and at best, marginally satisfactory. At the very least it put a certain physicality to the ending of a very, very brief relationship.

Putting the iPhone into the cup holder, I leaned my forehead against the steering wheel and blew out a long breath. The smell of recent sex and Carlos' cologne filled my nose; I wasn't sure which was worse, the fact it was a cheap fragrance available at any corner drug store or the evidence that it had been an effective aphrodisiac. I'd no idea I could be seduced so inexpensively. Slowly, I pounded my head against the soft cover of the wheel a few times before starting up the SUV and squealing the tires on the concrete as I roared up the ramp to the street.

The streets were quiet as I drove back to my new condo; the rain had cleared up overnight, but the lights of the city blocked out any stars. Had I been wearing something a bit more substantial – or not in desperate need of a shower – the prospect of drowning my sorrows at one of the many twenty-four-hour diners was alluring. There was small comfort in knowing there were as many as there were, though. For it was the first rule of policework: know where you can grab a cup of coffee and a bite to eat no matter the time of day, since you never knew how long you might be out on the job.

A little after four in the morning, I re-entered the glass walled shower of my condo, the control twisted as far to Hell as I could manage. Plunging my head beneath the intensely hot water, I reached up and undid my ponytail, letting it loose as I closed my eyes and tried to forget the last several hours. My shower gel did little to wash away the displeasure I felt at my actions, but it *did* manage to finally erase the last vestiges of Carlos from my skin. It was a tiny victory of sorts, one that I held onto as I started to massage shampoo into my hair. Rinsing it out and then repeating the actions with the conditioner started to reset my general outlook on life; another fifteen minutes of simply letting the hot water cascade over me belatedly made me wonder if my neighbors below were wondering if something had sprung a leak above them.

I realized I didn't care at all and sat under the waterfall head for another few minutes, luxuriating in the feeling. That lasted until I remembered I *still* didn't have any towels; shaking off the worst of the water before exiting the shower, I padded into the master bedroom to dig out a set of sweats, grimacing as the fabric invariably clung to still-soggy portions of my body. They were well worn and normally about-the-house attire, but my rumbling stomach reminded me that other than pretzels on the final leg of my trip out, I'd not eaten a full meal for almost a day. Passing by that final diner had been too much; grabbing my keys, I was back on the road again, retracing my route.

Pulling into a parking lot of a diner clearly from another era – if not another planet – I squeezed the SUV into the final open spot, marveling that so many people would be looking for breakfast at six in the morning. On a Saturday, no less. Sliding out the driver's side, I wandered down a wide but short sidewalk that hugged massive glass windows displaying the patrons to the passing traffic; the effect seemed accentuated by the fly-away angled roof just above them, and the fabulously tacky neon lights tucked into the trim. It made me wonder if I would find waitresses wearing pastel uniforms, tri-cornered hats and white aprons inside.

As it turned out, I wasn't far off; both the waiters *and* waitresses wore what to my untrained eye appeared to be period-appropriate outfits. The woman who walked me to a booth against the window seemed old enough to have been there when the place started, but I was reluctant for some reason to ask her what year that was.

"Drew will be your server, hon," she said as she slid a pencil into what looked like a beehive hairdo.

I nodded and slid across the plastic-covered bench, critically reviewing the menu. Nothing on it appealed to me in the least, making me wonder why I'd even come.

"Good morning," I heard from the aisle. "I'm Drew. Coffee?"

"Yes," I said without looking up, "and a side order of cardiac arrest. Is there anything on this menu that's not fried?"

The chuckle of delight made me turn, and I found myself taking in my waiter. He was tall, dark haired and pierced in visible places that made me cringe while simultaneously wondering what he might be hiding beneath his outfit. One side of his hair had been cut long, nearly shoulder length, while the other was a buzz cut. His smile was warm and genuine, and as he spoke again, I realized he was wearing contacts that made his entire eye look like one big, black, pupil.

"Not much, I'm afraid," he chuckled again. "However," he added, lowering his voice confidentially, "we have a secret menu that's a bit healthier."

"Oh?" I asked. "Please tell me it has oatmeal and fresh blueberries."

Drew laughed. "Blueberries are out of season here," he smiled, "but how about raspberries?"

"I'll take what I can get," I said. "Sourdough toast?"

"You bet. Jam or Peanut butter?"

"Peanut butter."

Drew scribbled my order down on his pad and looked over it at me. "Swimmer?"

I blinked. "Yes," I said cautiously. "Why do you ask?"

"I am, too. And this is essentially what all of us order right after our morning workout."

"No kidding," I smiled. "Is there a team nearby? I've just moved to town and need to transfer."

Drew nodded as he poured my coffee from a carafe he'd been holding. "Practice is weekday mornings at the high school, five sharp; six on Saturday. We're always recruiting new members, so you should check us out."

"That's perfect," I smiled.

"I'll jot down the address for you before you go," he smiled back, and I got a brief flash when the spike in his tongue caught the light. "Welcome to California!"

"I grew up here, actually," I corrected. "I'm recently back. For work."

"Cool," he said, accepting it with the Zen of a...

"Surfer?" I asked.

"You know it," he smiled wider. He paused a beat. "I'm off at seven and heading to catch a wave after. Come with?"

"I don't have my board," I equivocated. "I literally arrived last night."

"I'll spot you," he said. "You look kinda tense. The ocean would do you good."

I started to object; between the files sitting on my breakfast nook, my need to procure laundry appliances – and some sort of furniture for the condo, for that matter – I already had a sense of what I *should* have been doing with my day. Glancing at my sweats, I wondered if Chief Andrews had a loose definition of Business Casual. Somehow, I doubted it, and added my general lack of professional attire to my burgeoning shopping list. "I don't have a wetsuit, either."

Drew stepped back and nodded slowly. "I think I have one that will fit." He paused and added with a slight smirk. "Like a glove."

Seriously? I thought to myself, trying not to roll my eyes. *Two in twenty-four hours?* "Uh... look, I--"

"Back in a jiff with your meal," he said and was gone.

As I sat there in the booth, alone, I realized I was *truly* alone for the first time in years. Sure, I had family a short distance away, but I was loath to come up with any excuse to interact with them. Outside of Sean and Deidre, then later Suzanne, there were just a handful of people I'd even *considered* a friend; most were fellow teammates at the pool or colleagues at the station. I didn't expect any of them to reach out now that I was in California, especially since I'd essentially just disappeared.

Much like Sean, I'd run across the drawbridge and pulled it up behind me. Or burned it.

Drew returned with a larger carafe of coffee and a small duffel he put down on the bench beside me. "Here's the suit," he said happily. "Try it on in the restroom and if it fits, you're welcome to keep it until you get yours."

"Thanks," I said, arching an eyebrow. "Are you always this friendly to strangers?"

"Absolutely," he laughed. "It's one way to make sure I get a large tip."

Despite the warning bells in my head, I sighed, resigned, grabbed the suit and sought out the restroom.

In the end, it had taken no small amount of tugging, wriggling and cursing to get into the otherwise flexible neoprene; saying it was form fitting was a colossal understatement. Had I been wearing a swim brief beneath it (which was my normal procedure), it was likely the logo would have been visible against the fabric. As it was, I was a tad worried it was more revealing than I wanted, but after managing to get into the thing (despite the stall in the restroom not being particularly accommodating of my six-foot-two frame), turning down the gift would have been an unnecessary insult to my new friend.

Opting not to fight it a second time, I pulled my sweats on over it and made my way back to the booth, where my breakfast was similarly just arriving. Drew's eyes went to the tiny portion of the suit exposed at my wrist and smiled. "I take it that's a yes," he said.

I nodded as I slid into the booth, pulling down the top of my sweatshirt to show him more. "I guess I'll just have to surf this morning," I laughed as I let the collar slip back. "Especially since I'm not sure I'll be able to get back out of it. It's kind of tight."

"Good," he said, his eyes dancing with merriment. "That's what I was hoping."

Arching an eyebrow as I picked up a spoon, I asked: "That the suit is tight? Or that I'm going to the beach?" *With you,* I didn't add.

"Yes," he laughed. "I'll check on you in a bit."

-- ---- --

The tide was perfectly turning when we arrived at the beach, the parking lot about half-full with people clad just as I was in diverse colors of neoprene, though black seemed to be predominant. Most were hauling boards off their rooftop holders or pulling them from a trunk or flatbed; I felt a little awkward sliding the unmarked SUV in next to the beat-up Chevy truck that was Drew's ride and simply stepping out, waiting for my benefactor. With the deftness borne from years of practice, he quickly shucked out of his street clothes and into a wetsuit that was nearly identical to my borrowed one – all beneath a single towel, held with one hand, in the shadow of his truck. It took me back to my own years on the beach as a teen.

Hauling two short boards from the back of his truck, he handed me one before we started across the wide sandy beach toward the crashing waves. The sky was a deep, deep blue, and cloudless after the rain. Coming across the shore at almost the perfect angle, the onshore wind was generating gentle swells just regularly enough that breakers were appearing every fourth or fifth cycle. Though it had been years since I'd been in the Pacific, all of my old senses immediately kicked in as I plotted the most efficient path out to the staging point; diving in, the cold of the water revitalized me in a way I'd long forgotten was possible.

By eleven, I knew the sun's reflection off of the water had given me the beginning of a bad sunburn on my face but didn't care. Trudging back up to the sand, I flopped down beside my board, pleasantly exhausted. Drew dropped to his knees beside me. "Dude," he said with some awe. "You have some *moves* out there."

"I spent more time than I care to admit on a beach much like this one, just up the coast," I said, folding my hands behind my head. "I'd forgotten how intoxicating the rhythm of the surf can be."

"Word," he said solemnly.

The sunbaked warmth of the sand filtered through the neoprene, and I closed my eyes for a moment to simply enjoy the sounds of life around me. It had warmed into a pleasant bookend to the holiday weekend, and the sand around me had become crowded with activity. I could hear a beach volleyball game going on behind me, and kids off in the distance arguing as to the exact height of their sandcastle's parapets. A stray whistle from a lifeguard had me pop open an eye; I'd had that gig the summer before my senior year, and as they say, once a guard, always a guard. Satisfied no one was drowning, I shifted to my side and looked at my companion.

Drew had unzipped the upper part of his wetsuit, rolling the top to his waist and exposing a well-tanned torso that was hairless, tattooed and pierced about where I had expected. He'd propped up his surfboard and was leaning his head against it, hands laced over his bellybutton, as those strange pupil-less eyes scanned the crashing surf. "Are you from around here?" I asked.

"Yeah," he said. "Kind of. I grew up in Los Angeles, but I live in the OC now."

I nodded, hearing the shorthand most Southern Californian's used for Orange County, that thin strip of wealth that sat between LA and Riverside. Rancho Linda relied on some services from the OC Sheriff, that much I knew from my interview. "Forgive me," I said, "but you don't seem like the typical resident of the OC."

He shifted slightly to face me, and the small ankh pendant I'd not caught earlier slid down a chiseled pec. Considering how I had spent my evening prior, I was somewhat impressed at the vague stirrings of arousal. "And what would that be?" he asked, the playful smile telling me he was aware of the effect he was having.

"Oh, I don't know. White? Hundred-dollar haircut? No piercings?"

That made him laugh. "I see you *are* from the area," he replied. "I'm a grad student at Cal State Irvine. Master's in Economics."

My eyes widened. "At the risk of repeating my earlier potential insult..."

Drew laughed again. "Yeah, I don't fit the mold of a typical data wonk, as my faculty advisor reminds me on a regular basis." He sighed a bit. "It doesn't help I'm on the five-year plan, either. But I should graduate next fall."

I did the math and realized he potentially was close to my age. "What keeps distracting you?" I asked.

"Life," he smiled again as he waved at the ocean. "And the allure of the surf." He paused, looking back at me. "Beautiful strangers crossing my path."

I rolled my eyes. "That is the *worst* pickup line I've ever heard."

He leaned in, close enough I could smell his sweat intermingled with the tang of the salt water. It was, oddly, enthralling. "The real question is, did it work?"

"Look, I don't want you to get the wrong impression," I replied. "I'm not looking for anything solid at the moment. Not yet."

"Good," he smiled. "Neither am I." His strange eyes held mine for a long moment. "You look like you could really use a friend. Maybe even one with benefits."

Startled a bit that he had read me so well, I smiled to cover my embarrassment. "Is it that obvious?"

"Dude, you were sitting in my diner at six on a Saturday, wearing nothing but sweats. If that doesn't say you're on the rebound from something awful, I don't know what does."

I blinked again, unsure of how he'd managed to land two shots to my soul. "Economics? Are you sure you're not going into counseling?"

Drew laughed. "There's little money in Econ, but even less in Counseling." He sat up and said, very carefully, "I need to rinse off this salt. You?"

"Yes," I replied, and paused for a moment before throwing caution to the wind again. "And I know a good shower," I added, "if you're interested."

Standing, he caught my eye again. "Very," was his two-syllable reply.

Four

Given how much time I'd spent in my new shower over my first one-and-a-half days, I worried slightly that my neighbors might make a ruckus with the leasing agent. Nevertheless, Drew and I discovered the glass-walled enclosure was comfortable for two, with the added bonus of facing the massive mirror over the dual sinks. My very thorough attention to detail uncovered several more piercings, one of which truly made me cringe but didn't appear to cause him any pain. There was also an intriguing tattoo of a small cat on his hip that was a bit of an outlier, given the Emo/punk rock vibe of the rest of his ink. I'd been forced to file that question away for later, for he returned the favor, and then some.

We parted ways after a late lunch at the In-N-Out just a few blocks from my place.

"Thank you for a great re-introduction to SoCal," I smiled as we stood beside our respective vehicles in the parking lot. "As you might have noted, I don't have much in the condo – I appreciate you loaning me some towels, by the way; I'll get them washed up and returned the next time I'm at the diner."

"I'm not worried."

"I know," I laughed. "Since I also don't have anything to cook with, either, I'll be a frequent customer at the diner for a bit."

Drew smiled. "Good. I have third shift, so that would be an excellent way to end my day," he said, before adding: "Sadly, I'm off on Mondays and Wednesdays."

"That's a shitty weekend."

"It's the price I pay for flexibility," he replied. "Besides, it gives me time on the beach when everyone else is slogging away at their nine-to-five."

"No kidding," I laughed as he climbed into his beat-up truck. I waited until he rolled down the window. "See you tomorrow?"

"I'll be there," he nodded. "The tide is not going to be as good in the morning, though. If you want to catch some waves, it might have to be closer to the afternoon."

"Works for me." I waved as he pulled out, then slid into my unmarked SUV.

The mid-to-late afternoon was spent doing what I'd planned on doing before being distracted by the beach: wandering a mall I'd located close to the pool for the swim team Drew had recommended, picking up condo necessities. Given how much it cost me to get sufficient kitchen items, a washer and dryer, towels in a variety of sizes and several sets of polos and matching khakis, I was silently thankful my bank account was fairly healthy. Living expenses back in Windeport had been minimal, given that Sean refused to charge me rent; aside from groceries, he'd never let me pay a dime toward utilities or any other expense. Though my virtual wallet took quite a hit that afternoon, I still had plenty on hand to survive for nearly a year should I find myself unemployed unexpectedly.

The appliances and my new California King bed couldn't be delivered before mid-week; everything else required multiple trips from the parking garage. Somewhere close to seven, I leaned against the breakfast bar and finally cracked open my first beer from my newly supplied fridge, then silently toasted to new beginnings. Sipping at the bitter but welcome hops in my Samuel Adams, I wondered if my first week in California would be as eventful as the first two days had turned out to be. Yawning, I wasn't entirely sure I'd be able to keep up the pace, not without getting a few hours of shuteye.

My iPhone took that moment to buzz, sliding across the counter as it did so. Looking down, I saw it was a familiar number, one that I'd not yet had the heart to delete. But I also knew I was far from ready to talk to him. Deleting the text without reading it, I flipped the phone upside down and took another long swig from the bottle.

Sean's text drew my eyes to the files that were still on the countertop, and the laptop that was open but locked. As I stood in front of the mess, a wave of guilt washed over me for not prioritizing the case review. If Sean had been the one asking, I'd have already sent him the summary and my initial conclusions; Chief Andrews wouldn't be able to get so much as a vague opinion on it from me at this point.

What the hell is wrong with me? I wondered, taking another pull from the beer. *I've spent more time "playing" than being the cop he hired.*

My iPhone buzzed again. Sighing, I flipped it up and deleted the follow-up text from Sean. Clearly, he'd missed the whole "don't call me" part of our conversation in the hallway at Maine Medical Center, or he was treating texting as a loophole large enough to drive his concern for my wellbeing through. Back on the lock screen of my phone, I dithered again, for even with the mountains of guilt I felt, I had zero desire to dig into it that evening.

Screw it, I thought, wondering where this rebellious part of myself was coming from. Less than twenty minutes later and several hundred dollars lighter, I found myself walking along the packed Main Street of Disneyland, working my way around people who were even then, two hours before the event, staking out prime locations to watch the nightly fireworks. My interests lay elsewhere, though I wondered if I would be able to pull off my little legerdemain.

I hadn't counted on the heavier-than-normal crush of visitors to the park, owing to the Thanksgiving holiday, so it took far more effort to navigate across the park. Like a beacon shining in the night, though, I finally arrived at a nondescript door in New Orleans Square. The number thirty-three was affixed to it, and a small doorbell/speaker combo mounted just to the side. Smiling, I pressed the button.

"Good evening, sir," was the prompt response. "What guest name is the reservation under?"

"Korsokovach," I replied. "Vasily Korsokovach. And I don't have a reservation this evening. Is there space at the bar?"

There was a long pause. "Of course, sir. Step through, please."

The door clicked open, and it pulled easily toward me on well-oiled hinges; as I looked around the perfectly themed small lobby, I smiled at the tiny details that had gone into the hidden gem most Disneyland guests had no idea was buried inside one of the most famous attractions in the world. Looking to the small concierge desk, I smiled. "Giovanni," I said as I reached for his hand. "It's been a while."

"Indeed, sir," the older gentleman replied from behind the counter, smiling. His full head of hair was grey now, reflecting his long tenure as the gatekeeper. "What brings you to Anaheim? Your parents didn't mention you were in town."

"Work, actually," I answered, though my stomach lurched a bit at the thought of my family. "How's Daniel?"

"My youngest is finishing up his residency in reconstructive plastic surgery at UCLA," he said proudly. "I expect he'll land in a practice next spring."

"I'm impressed," I said, not wanting to mention his son may or may not have encouraged his boyfriend at the time to help him with his Senior Biology anatomy lessons. "I lost track of him after he went into the Peace Corps. I've not talked to him in a while."

"Well," Giovanni smiled, "it's good to see you. This way, please," he said, holding out his hand.

"I'm glad you could find me a spot. Coming in was a spur-of-the-moment decision."

Giovanni smiled again as he pressed the button for the small lift enclosed in wrought iron cage. "We always have space for our most loyal members," he replied with practiced ease.

"Of course. Well, thanks just the same."

We chatted companionably for the short ride to the second floor, but I paused when he turned left, and I turned right. "I'm sorry," I smiled, a bit perplexed. "I know it's been a while, but Isn't the bar this way?"

"It is," Giovanni smiled. "But your party is *this* way."

"My... party?" I said falteringly.

Giovanni just smiled and waited for me patiently to catch up.

The tiny lurch of my stomach became something more like acid indigestion, erasing all desire for the Monte Cristo sandwich I'd planned on ordering. "They're here?"

"Yes," Giovanni nodded. "And you're here as their *guest*," he added with subtle emphasis.

"Ah," I nodded. "When did I come off the rolls, exactly?" I asked, knowing it took an act of God to remove a member from Club Thirty-Three, owing to the fact membership was generally for life.

"Fifteen years ago," he replied quietly. "Now, if you please..." he said, extending his hand toward the dining room.

Feeling a bit like the outcast teenager I'd been while living in California, I tried to plaster a smile on my face as we crossed the small dining room to a table in the corner. As I approached the couple who were sitting at a four top, reviewing the case suddenly seemed like it had been a better option than a nostalgic trip down memory lane of the life I'd once had.

My mother caught my figure first, and her well-schooled features didn't betray anything other than the faux look of surprise at my unexpected appearance. Her hair was expensively done as I remembered it, carefully colored to hide any traces of time. Makeup hid the worst of the age lines, but not all of them, and I could see that she'd put back on the thirty pounds she'd lost the year I came out.

Papa had his face buried in the menu, which in itself was a message, given it hadn't changed appreciatively in decades. His hair had thinned enough that his spotted pate was quite visible, testament to the long hours he apparently continued to spend on the golf course. His gin and tonic – long a staple in the Korsokovach household – was sitting just out of reach of his hand, the condensation beginning to form along the exterior of the tumbler. I wondered if it was his second, or a third to drown out the pain of my appearance.

Both were dressed to the nines, as was more or less appropriate to the rarefied atmosphere of the club. I saw my mother's eyes take in my ponytail, polo and khakis with a small moue of disapproval playing around her lips. Neither stood as Giovanni introduced me, pulled out a chair, and then left me to my execution.

"Mama," I said as I pulled the napkin from the plate and folded it into my lap. "Papa."

"Your hair. Is too long still," she said, her heavy accent still present despite the decades she and Papa had been citizens.

"It's good to see you too," I smiled without warmth.

"When did you get back into town?" Papa asked. Years of running an almost-Fortune 500 company had knocked the worst of *his* accent away, but he, too, had traces of his upbringing in Ukraine – if you knew what to listen for.

I smiled, for his question had the matter-of-fact tone that told me it was for form only; the actual response didn't matter. "A while ago."

"How long staying?" Mama asked, her clipped syllables underscoring her discomfort.

From her, I knew the question had more to do with whether she felt like another round of apologizing to her social circle for the aberrant behavior of her son was in order; given my current age, it seemed comical that it was still an issue.

Then again, maybe not.

"A while," I repeated, shrugging. "I'm sorry to surprise you like this. I didn't realize I wasn't on the membership any longer, nor did I know you'd be here."

"You had no use for it in Maine," Papa replied as he put down the menu. His eyes skipped around the room, looking at everything but me as I sat across from him, a pattern that had started immediately after my disclosure. "Not that it saves us any money."

"Well, I'm happy to pay for my meal this evening, if it helps," I quickly replied, intending to be insulting. The flame of anger on my father's face told me I'd scored a direct hit, given how he abhorred being reminded of his salad years.

"Dat von't be necessary," Mama replied, her faux smile still trained on me as she reached for her wineglass. "Our treat."

"How kind," I smiled.

The waiter blissfully appeared, one I didn't recognize from the early days, took our orders and disappeared. We sat in stony silence, our mutual aggrievements inappropriate discussion material for Club Thirty-Three. Papa continued to ignore that I was even in the room, let alone sitting at his table; Mama was just the opposite, never letting her gaze stray too far from me. I knew she had been the one to overrule Papa when the call had come up from the door on the first floor, though I could also see she was now reconsidering the wisdom of having allowed me in.

My thoughts ping-ponged between thousands of hours of meals like this pre- and post-coming out; I knew I came from wealth, hard earned by Papa as he'd climbed the corporate ladder. I also knew I'd never see a dime of *any* of it; my trust fund and any inheritance I might have had were forfeit not long after their final failure to talk me out of being gay. I shook my head, trying not to cringe at how we three had acted with each other; the anger, the shouting. The crying. Lots and lots of crying, and not just from my mother.

The UEM scholarship had been my ticket away on multiple levels, not the least of which was financial independence. Without my trust fund, a full-ride was my only chance to attend any college on my own terms, and most of my first choices hadn't rolled out the red carpet. I remembered arriving in Windeport carrying the anger and burden of being excommunicated from my family; those early days alone would have been much darker had the swim team not collectively circled the wagons around me.

Had Sean not come into my life.

Somehow, we managed to make it to the after-dessert coffee without killing anyone. As I sipped the robust brew, I decided to poke the bear slightly. Clearing my throat, I announced with no fanfare: "I'll swing by next weekend to pick up a few things, if that's all right."

"Dings?" Mama said, panic that I would actually grace their driveway evident in her face. "Vat dings?"

"My surf gear, for one. Books, movies. Clothes. Personal items. That kind of thing."

"Vasily, there's nothing for you at the house," Papa said quietly.

"You put it into storage?" I asked. "Geez, Papa, I've not been gone *that* long."

"No," he replied, finally looking me in the eye.

I felt my face heat up. "You... you sold my stuff?"

"No," he replied again, and for the first time he betrayed the slightest emotion. A glint of satisfaction appeared in his eyes. "We burned it. All of it."

"You... *what*?!" I breathed, anger tempered by incredulousness.

"We don't have a son any longer," Papa said as he shifted his gaze to something over my shoulder and raised a hand. "He's been gone for a long, long time. There was no need to keep anything to remind us of our... loss."

"*I'm right here*," I said tightly through gritted teeth. "I'm not dead! You had no right--"

A hand appeared at my shoulder, and I turned to see Giovanni smiling down at me sadly. "Thank you for joining us," he said pleasantly. "Unfortunately, the fireworks viewing is for members only. I'll have to ask you to leave, now."

"Right," I said hotly as I tossed the napkin onto the table and stood. "Thank you for dinner," I managed to spit out reasonably politely.

Both parents looked away.

"This way, please," Giovanni said with the faux pleasantry all Disney Cast Members were trained in, trying to take me by the arm.

"I am well aware of where the exit is," I snapped, shaking him off and moving deliberately across the room to the stairs. As I exited the ornate doorway back into the theme park proper, I took a deep breath to try and shore up my emotions.

They say you can never go home again. As the door to Club Thirty-Three clicked shut with finality, it seemed to me it was true. The real question was whether I'd really wanted to or not in the first place.

As I walked the crowded pathway, I decided I hadn't.

FIVE

I'd been overly optimistic with respect to sleeping on the carpet in the master bedroom; despite outward appearances, the flooring did not appear to be as upscale as other, more visible aspects of the condo. Sleep, when it came, was fitful at best, and by four I was awake with no desire to try for another hour. My body was still somewhat on East Coast time, so I dug through my duffel to come up with my running gear; when I pushed through the door to Katella Avenue, the chilly early morning air wiped away any last cobwebs from my brain.

Stretching slightly, I started off toward Disneyland, the map of Anaheim in my mind. I had no specific route planned other than possibly winding up at the diner just as Drew wrapped his shift. That seemed a stretch goal at best, and as I felt myself warm up, realized putting in a long run when I was also planning on hitting the waves again later might not be the best plan of action. In the end I did a small loop that brought me back to the building while still covering close to three miles; that felt like enough of a victory for me to go directly to the garage and head for some breakfast.

Had I been honest with myself, I wasn't as interested in eating as I was in having a friendly ear. Dinner with my parents weighed heavily on my mind, dredging up all sorts of issues I thought had been buried deep never to be seen again. Clearly that wasn't true; they treated me as the pariah they clearly viewed me to be, and the quasi-public humiliation had only served to underscore their point. That it could still make me angry was more the issue; I'd long gotten over being, essentially, forcefully emancipated from the family name. What last night had shown me was they both still had the ability to cut me to the quick, despite my feeling of invulnerability.

What irked me more – still irked me, actually – was their continuing view that it somehow had been a *choice* for me, which to their everlasting shame I'd made incorrectly. It wasn't, of course, but that hadn't stopped them from trying to make me feel as though it was somehow reversible, that I could simply uncheck a box as if swapping political parties.

As if it were that simple.

The same grandmotherly host met me at the diner. She got a half smile when she saw me in running tights and a lightweight pullover, almost as if I had confirmed something in her mind. I tried not to roll my eyes; save for the long hair, I'd never felt like I was the flamboyant type. Choking back a sarcastic comment, I instead greeted her. "Bit chilly this morning, isn't it?"

"It will be all week," she counseled as she took me toward the same booth I'd had the day earlier. As she handed me my menu, she smiled toothily. "I pegged you as an athlete yesterday."

"Really?" I replied, thrown a little before joking: "I suppose the leggings are a dead giveaway."

"It didn't hurt," she laughed. "No, it was the way you hold your body. We get a lot of the kids from the local high school and CSUI sporting teams here after practice. You all walk the same way."

"Interesting observation," I nodded.

"No charge," she said. "Drew will be your server today, but you already knew that. Enjoy your meal, hon."

I fiddled with the menu for a moment before looking out to the street and watching the traffic. Even on Sunday morning it was a steady flow in both directions; come Monday, I'd see commuter traffic for the first time in, well, ages. I had to admit, the short five-minute commute from Sean's apartment to the Public Safety building had truly spoiled me.

"Hey," I heard over my shoulder, and I turned with a smile to see Drew. "You look like shit."

"Thanks," I said. "You might recall I had no furniture when you were over; I'm sleeping on my rug until Wednesday."

"I was paying attention to other things," he smirked. "But that sounds awful."

"It's just for another night or two. I've done worse."

He nodded. "So you were a Boy Scout, too?"

"Hell, no," I laughed. "I didn't have time for anything quite so pedestrian."

"Are you mocking my Eagle?" Drew asked good naturedly.

"Not in the least." I flipped the menu back toward him. "Same as yesterday, I guess. And would you mind hitting the beach earlier than we'd agreed? I really do have to get some work done before I report in tomorrow."

Scribbling on his pad, Drew nodded. "The surf won't be as good," he warned, "but I'm pretty open today. Sure."

"I appreciate it."

He eyed me. "Let me get this order started and then I'll be out with coffee." He leaned closer. "And then you can tell me what happened."

I sighed. "Is it that obvious I need someone to talk to?"

"Yeah," he replied with a half-smile. "But maybe we'll wait until we're on the water," he added after a moment. "I feel like this will take more than the normal two minutes of witty banter waiters typically allow."

That made me laugh. "Quite likely, yes."

"Then I will expedite this order and make sure I can punch out on time."

-- ---- --

I had thought to stash the wetsuit in my truck, so once Drew's shift had ended, we caravanned directly to the beach for the second day in a row, nearly scoring the exact same spots in the lot. To my surprise, there were far more Sun Worshippers for a Sunday than I expected, but we still found a patch of shore to call our own. Diving in once more, I paddled out into the anemic swells and then sat up on the board, hanging my feet off either side and into the cold Pacific.

Drew angled himself next to me, and we were essentially alone; the true surfers had looked up the forecast as he had and wouldn't appear until later. It was oddly serene sitting two hundred yards from shore, gently bobbing up and down as swells rolled beneath us, casually pushing us a few feet closer to the sand.

"Out with it," he said as he stroked a bit to stay even with my board.

I sighed, and looked across the shoreline for a long moment. "I ran into my folks last night," I began. "I wasn't expecting to, and they had no idea I'd returned to California. It was something of a shock for all of us."

"Ouch."

"Yeah. I wound up having dinner with them – that was the only saving grace, I suppose, getting a delicious meal out of them. The rest of the evening I could have skipped without any issue."

"Why?"

I sighed again. "Can I ask you a personal question?"

"Sure."

"How did your family react when you came out?"

Drew shrugged, the neoprene rippling slightly in the sunlight as he did. "I dunno if I'm the right person to ask."

My eyes widened, and I wondered if I had misread him completely. "Dude... are you not...?" I asked, trailing off. "I mean... in the shower it seemed like...?"

That made him laugh. "I swing both ways, if that's what you're trying to ask. As it happens, this week I'm swinging in your particular direction."

I closed my eyes and could feel a headache coming on. Man, I could really pick 'em.

"Dad was the same way before he settled down with Tom," Drew continued. "I come by it naturally." He paddled his board around to face me. "When Dad split with Mom, I was six; Tom became my second father when I was eight. It was all very amicable – I still see Mom from time to time – so to be honest, my own situation was pretty well received." He laughed again. "I think my problem is that I feel like I'm missing out if I were to choose one side or the other. So I haven't. Yet."

"Wow."

"Well, what works for us doesn't necessarily mean it would for anyone else. And I'm thinking your family falls into that latter category."

"Totally," I replied. "I knew who I was at ten," I started, watching as a seagull flew overhead. "But I also knew how my parents would react. So I was that kid, the one who tried *not* to be who he was."

"That sucks."

"Yeah," I nodded. "And as an athlete, I had extra pressure to conform and be 'normal,' whatever that means."

Drew nodded. "Swimming, right?"

"Yeah," I smiled. "How could you tell?"

He flushed a bit. "I'd like to say it was because of your classic 'v' shaped torso, but I Googled you when you paid the bill yesterday. I thought I recognized the name."

I rolled my eyes. "You're not the first one," I laughed.

"Sorry."

"Don't apologize. You're still talking to me reasonably normally; that's a win for me. Half the time I find people only sidle up to me to be close to someone famous. What's worse is I'm about ten orbits out of famous at this point."

"Maybe," he smiled. "What did you mean by normal? Normal to them?"

"Pretty much," I sighed again. "It came crashing down when I turned sixteen, though. I'd managed to keep my relationships off the radar at my high school, but I slipped up just once."

"Oh God," he said. "I'm not sure I want to know what happened."

"You don't," I said, unwilling to actually tell him. "Without going into particulars, at sixteen I suddenly found my future was boxed in a bit. I wound up on a full-ride to a small school in Maine; it was my salvation, and a ticket to the Olympics."

"Rough, dude. And last night was the first time you'd seen them since leaving?"

"Yeah." I wrung out my hair and tied it loosely off my neck; the sun was getting a bit warm. "Do you watch *Star Trek*?"

"Are you kidding?" he laughed. "It was required television in my household."

"You know that thing that happens to Worf? When he essentially falls on his sword for his family and gets publicly shamed with the ritual of discommendation?"

"I do," he said, nodding. "He did an honorable thing to hide another's dishonor to keep the Empire from fraying."

"That's me, essentially," I laughed ruefully, "save for keeping the Empire together. I really don't have a family any longer, which was emphasized pointedly last night."

"That's nuts!"

"That's my family in a nutshell."

We sat there for a while, gently rising and falling with the swells. I'd not noticed the small pier that jutted out into the ocean on our prior visit; I'm sure it had been there, of course, but I'd been so focused on getting into the water and getting Carlos out of my brain it hadn't registered. As Sunday morning rolled on, I could see there was some sort of antique auto show taking place along its length, though I wasn't entirely able to see the wide variety of models on offer; several dozen people had lines over the edge, catching God knew what in the waters below. I'm not sure I'd have been brave enough to eat anything pulled from the Pacific along the coast, given the visible refinery a few miles up the beach, but then again, here I was paddling along blissfully in the same water.

I blinked and realized those were domes more indicative of nuclear power, and wondered if I'd just forfeited any chance of having kids of my own. I took a small measure of comfort that California, of any state, would be on top of monitoring plants such as that for any sort of emissions. But the fear lingered for a moment longer, unresolved.

"This looks to be a bust for surfing," Drew said at length.

"I cut my run short just in case, too," I said regretfully. "So much for getting my exercise today."

Drew smiled. "Let's see what we can do about that, then," he replied as he started to paddle toward the shore.

"Someone is feeling frisky," I called after his receding form.

"From the moment you appeared in the diner..."

-- ---- --

Considering his outward appearance, Drew's apartment was a comfortable, cozy studio on the far side of Rancho Linda. Unlike my place, though, the shower was nearly claustrophobic for two, resulting in some very intriguing gymnastics that were more than a little eye-opening for me. Close to the noon hour, I found myself pleasantly exhausted and, finally, somewhat at peace; towel wrapped around my waist, I was laying along his couch watching the exotic color of his back while he mixed something in the kitchenette.

"What are you doing over there?" I asked, pushing back the tiny voice in my brain reminding me I still had hours of work ahead of me.

"Creating a proper cocktail to finish off the morning," he said as he turned and headed across to me carrying two tumblers. "This is the drink of the Raj."

"The *who*?" I asked as I accepted the glass. Eyeing it, the liquid inside was clear but carbonated.

"The Raj? Come on, you were a 3.5 GPA student after all. You must have had World History at UEM?"

I smiled at him slightly. "It's a bit freaky how much you know about me."

He shrugged. "The internet is an amazing thing, man." He held up the glass. "My father – well, my biological father, not Tom – taught me that this drink is fit for the Raj; that would be the equivalent of a king, I suppose, in the land of my forebears. It is a gin and tonic, made with only the best: Bombay Sapphire."

I looked at Drew again and connected the olive complexion, dark hair and, without the contacts, even darker pupils. "India?"

"Right on, dude," he smiled. "Though not for several generations now. But genealogy is important to Dad, so I know that I'm connected to a royal caste known for their technical skills."

"Wow," I said. "Impressive. I'm not even descended from Russian nobility, minor or otherwise."

"Nobody's perfect," he laughed as he held up his glass. "Cheers."

Six

I spent far longer than I should have with Drew, getting back to my condo in the dregs of Sunday afternoon. As it turned out, he was a fascinating individual, with a richly complex family and an insanely curious mind hiding beneath his surfer persona. I knew the sex between us was casual, but also felt cautiously optimistic that a solid friendship was forming, something I knew I needed if I were ever to create the fresh start I was craving in California.

After re-rinsing out my borrowed wetsuit, I hung it on one of the hooks in the so-called "surfer station" the property owner had installed for me in the half-bath laundry room. Consisting of two shelves that could hold surfboards above a set of hooks for soggy neoprene, it was something of a staple in beach homes in California; it was certainly more practical than slinging the salt-encrusted suit over the top of the shower enclosure. The image in the small mirror over the sink reminded me I was still in my running gear; given how late in the day it was, and my lack of a washing machine, I figured it prudent to keep out of the clean clothes inventory for a bit longer – and there were certainly worse things to lounge around in than comfortable spandex.

Smiling at myself, I snapped off the light and moved back to the kitchen, then around to the breakfast bar and my MacBook. The files were still right where I left them, the laptop half-open but in electronic slumber. Waking the laptop, I signed in once more then moved around to the fridge so I could retrieve a chef's salad I'd picked up during my supply run on Saturday. I'd spent enough time around Sean that I'd developed some pretty decent skills in the kitchen, but just didn't feel up to anything that required massive cleanup later. Tearing the plastic off the top of the small tub, I realized not getting a television to connect to the U-verse system that came with the condo had been an oversight, especially since the Patriots were the late game. It was a mistake I'd fix on the way home tomorrow evening – hopefully in time to catch the Packers taking on the Bears.

Accessing the virtual casebook once more, I flipped back to the beginning and lost myself in the narrative of the file. Admittedly, I had only the experience of working under a single supervisor in a small department, but Sean had been nearly maniacal about following proper process and procedure. The casebooks from my time in Windeport had therefore been highly organized and overwhelmingly complete, down to the most minute of details. We'd followed a similar pattern when doing our consulting work across both Maine and the wider New England region, earning a reputation for quality work that consistently held up in court.

This file appeared to be anything but. Despite the software's best efforts to make the lead investigator conform to the S&Ps, I quickly found it had been a rather haphazard affair, with key steps of the investigation either incomplete or simply missing. It took me a full hour to realize there had only been a single, fifteen-minute interview with the author who had been burglarized; based on the transcript, there had *maybe* been a tentative agreement to circle back for a longer session, but that had never materialized. The dates pegged the first meeting a few days after the case was opened; now nearly a month old, getting accurate recollections from *anyone* would be a major problem.

Sipping my second Samuel Adams, I pushed back from the counter and wondered if this was some sort of odd hazing ritual the Chief was putting me through. I'd heard of such things, but our brief conversation from the airport left me with the impression he wasn't that kind of a commanding officer. There was also the fact he'd handed me the case days before my official start; that told me there was an urgency to uncovering a new lead, or some other agenda he'd not shared with me.

He is retiring, I thought to myself as I wandered to the patio doors. *Maybe he wants to balance out his accounts, clear his debts before he leaves. It's reasonable. And this is a bit of a high-profile case, too.*

Which it was, but why assign it to the new guy?

I turned back to the computer and flipped to the main screen for the casebook. The investigator was still listed as Mark Freidman; clicking onto his name dropped me into the department phonebook function, displaying his department-issued phone number. Checking the time to be sure I wasn't too late, I punched his number into my iPhone and dialed.

Two rings and he picked up. "Detective Freidman," came a deep baritone well suited for the stage.

"Detective, I'm sorry to call you on a Sunday. This is Vasily Korsokovach – I'm starting on Monday in the department?"

There was a pause. "The kid from Maine?"

"I don't know about the 'kid' part," I laughed for form, not at all liking the connotation. "But I am from Maine, yes."

There was a laugh to match from his side. "Kid, anyone younger than me is a kid."

I glanced at his bio in the phonebook. "I'm only four years younger, Detective."

"Call me Mark," he laughed. "What can I do for you on a Sunday?"

"I hope I'm not interrupting," I hedged.

"Not at all," he replied. "The Pats have more or less ground the Jets into the soil at this point."

"How bad?"

"Forty-nine to zero with ten minutes left in the third."

"Ouch."

"No kidding. That first round pick for the Fins must be wondering what he did wrong in life to get sent to Miami."

"Well, Chief Andrews asked me to look over the Frankenhoffer case before I reported for duty tomorrow. I see you were the lead investigator on it and wondered if you had any background you think I should know?"

"Oh Jesus," he said. "I wondered what happened to that albatross of a case."

"That sounds... awful."

"It was," he said. "Dr. Frankenhoffer – she insists you call her by her title – is about what you would expect from an entitled rich person. She was exceedingly difficult to work with."

"That's a bit unusual," I observed. "Especially if you were essentially working on her behalf."

"Which we were," he sighed, audible across the open connection. "I've got plenty I can share with you that's not in the file," he added. "It's not too late if you want to chat tonight. I'm hanging out at *Bar None* ostensibly watching the game."

That would be an improvement since there's hardly anything there, I thought to myself. "Sure. Text me the address and I'll be there."

-- ---- --

Bar None, despite its moniker, seemed like any other dive I had been in during my adult life. It fronted the main thoroughfare in Placentia, California, and finding a parking spot proved to be a challenge owing to Sunday Night Football. I wound up backing out of the small lot behind the building and circling the block until I found an open spot on a side street; the short walk gave me some time to order my thoughts before pushing in the glass door to the space.

The cacophony washed over me as I entered with multiple televisions blaring the Pats game; their volume was just slightly higher than the hubbub from the patrons, making me wonder where Mark had taken my call. I'd sent his official headshot to my iPhone, but that proved unnecessary, for as I started to push through the crowd, a solid, tall man detached himself from the bar and waved me over.

As I got closer, I could tell it was Mark, and I shook his outstretched hand. His grip was strong, and as I took him in from head to toe, I saw he had that classic chiseled jaw with high cheekbones that women (and some men) found attractive. His green eyes were a nice compliment to his expensively done hair; looking for all the world like he had rolled out of bed to join me, I knew for a fact it took a long time and an amazing amount of hair product to get the mussed-up look exactly right, having tried it myself many, many years earlier. I had a just enough wave to make it nearly impossible to pull off and had quickly grown it back out again to the shoulder-length I'd worn since high school.

Mark was wearing a t-shirt for what looked like a local rock band, with sweat stains at the arms owing to the warmth of the room; blue jeans hugged what I could see was a nicely shaped ass. Not knowing what to expect, I'd thrown my sweats on over my running gear and was suddenly quite conscious of the small rip above a knee exposing some of the tri-colored spandex beneath. I shrugged mentally, for bars had never really been my scene. I'd learned early on there was a connection between *where* I picked up someone and how fulfilling the experience ultimately turned out to be. Bars tended to be at the wrong end of the spectrum, filed in my mind under the "desperate for action" category.

Inclining his head, Mark indicated a small archway that appeared to lead to another section of the bar. I nodded and followed him as his considerable bulk snowplowed through the crowd. On the other side of the archway, the noise dropped noticeably. A single big-screen television had the game on, and Al Michaels appeared to be pontificating about some aspect of the game. I shrugged, thinking everything that could be said about Tom Brady had likely been said. I feared the day he left New England.

Mark slid into a booth that had two beers, matching napkins and what looked like potato skins. I matched his move on the opposite side as he said, "I ordered you a Corona. Well, technically, I ordered *me* a Corona – it's two for one through nine, so you get my spare."

"Thanks," I smiled, wondering if I should tell him I disliked Corona intensely. "I think."

"My pleasure." He took a swig from the glass bottle, sizing me up as he did so, but in a way that actually felt a bit invasive.

I'd often heard women who'd said they'd watched as their date had mentally undressed them, and until that moment, had never experienced it myself. This was an unexpected behavior from a colleague, though it *was* Sunday and he'd clearly been drinking. Hoping to derail whatever he was considering, I smiled. "How did you catch the case?"

"Dumb shit luck," he breathed. "I'd picked up a weekend watch for the overtime and happened to be the detective on duty when the body of the housekeeper was found. Twenty more minutes and it would have been the overnight guy."

"Walk me through it."

Mark snorted. "Not much to walk through. Housekeeper was an Asian in her late sixties, been with Frankenhoffer for decades. Head smashed by something round and heavy, though nothing at the scene matched that particular description; typical B-and-E, lots of high dollar items were missing. Perp went through the glass door to the room. Wide screen television, collectible art, the desktop computer, the family silver."

I shook my head. "The killer *took* the weapon?" I asked, for it was a tiny detail that had not been in the commentary for the file. I'd made that assumption, of course, since nothing had been found at the scene. Hearing Mark confirm it, though, made me uneasy for some reason.

"Seems that way," he said.

"I saw the crime scene photos. Do you think they surprised the housekeeper?"

"Position of the body supports that," he said.

"Forgive me, but that's not exactly a 'yes.'"

"No, it's not," he sighed, running a hand through his unkempt hair.

"I can't prove it – yet – but I think the poor woman didn't die where we found her. The wound to the head should have left quite a bit of blood behind, and while there was some, there just wasn't *enough* for my tastes."

I kept my face impassive, for even though Mark was the principal investigator, none of this had been in the file. "You must not have found anything to support that, then?"

"No," he shook his head. "But I know in my gut the body was moved."

"I don't recall seeing a subsequent search of the house in the file," I observed. "Certainly not for any sort of trace evidence like that."

"As tragic as the death of the housekeeper is, once the manuscript became the focus, her... situation was put on the back burner."

I blinked. "You... you shelved the murder investigation? Over a property theft?"

"Not by choice," he muttered. "The manuscript is worth ten million to the publisher."

My jaw gaped. "It's... it's *what?"*

Mark laughed. "Dr. Frankenhoffer is bank for her publisher. No title has sold less than a million copies; the advance they paid her for this last one is more than you or I will see in a lifetime on the force. To put it mildly, there is a lot riding on that lost book."

"Still," I said, feeling like the housekeeper deserved some recognition, "we're talking about someone taking someone else's *life*. Surely that could at least be a parallel investigation?"

Mark laughed again, a bit sardonically. "I don't know how they did things in your small-town department, but in Rancho Linda, budget drives every decision. We focus on the cases that affect the bottom line of the city; the ones that will let the Council continue to get re-elected on their 'safe community' platform."

"She's *dead*, Mark," I said, suddenly feeling more than a little annoyed the poor woman had been written off. "That has to mean something to someone."

"I'm sure it does. We just don't have the people to look into that *and* find the missing manuscript."

"That's--"

Mark looked at his watch. "Look, I'll go through the file with you more thoroughly tomorrow," he said, interrupting me. "Why don't we spend a little more time getting to know each other tonight?"

I saw *that* look in his eyes, and some major alarms triggered in the back of my head. Draining the last of my Corona, I smiled. "I'm still on East Coast time, actually. As much as I'd like to catch the last of the game, I'm gonna head home."

"Are you sure?" he asked.

"Some other time, maybe," I smiled wider as I slid to the edge of the booth. "Thanks for the beer."

"Anytime."

I wasn't sure why, but for some reason I wanted to bolt for the door; instead, I nodded, stood, and slowly escaped into the cool night air.

Seven

Drew had given me the address for the pool where the Masters Swim Team practiced, and though I'd initially thought of skipping out and just getting to the department at first light, the rational part of my brain reminded me a decent workout would calm my already jittery nerves considerably. After all, it had been more than ten years since I'd started a new gig; it was important to make a good first impression with my new colleagues, right?

Even if it seems they'd handed me a rather problematic case.

The high school was in Rancho Linda proper, just a few miles from the station according to Apple maps. I pulled into the parking lot beside the pool a bit before five, and unsurprisingly found it two-thirds full. A small queue had formed outside the gate leading into the pool, and I easily picked out Drew.

"Aren't you off today?" I asked as I walked over to him. "You could be sleeping in."

"I am," he smiled. "But this is my routine. Why break it? Come on, I'll introduce you to everyone."

Masters Swimming is essentially an umbrella organization, open to all who have an interest in swimming – whether as former competitors (such as myself) still wishing to chase a personal best time, or those who are fitness afficionados. Much like AA, every city has a branch, sometimes more than one, and you won't find a warmer, more welcoming environment anywhere in the sporting world. By the end of the workout that morning, it felt as though I had been part of the team for years, with multiple open-ended invitations to catch a drink or dinner. Save for the outdoor location of the venue, my team back in Maine had been virtually the same.

I caught a quick breakfast with Drew at the diner and still managed to arrive at the amazingly fortified gate to the lot at the Rancho Linda Police Department a fraction before seven. Given how suburban the city was, seeing the tall metal fencing arching over the street gave me pause. It was almost as if they were already planning for the eventual citizen revolt, complete with torches and pitchforks, at some point in the future. I tried to quash that as the officer at the gate analyzed my Maine ID and then waved me through.

Sliding the SUV into an open spot, I dug out the second sticky note Chief Andrews had given me with the code to the rear entrance. It was a bypass for use until I had my official ID; as it turned out, Mark Freidman was standing by said door, finishing the last of what smelled like a menthol cigarette.

"I hate to point this out," I smiled as I approached him. "But I'm pretty sure there was a sign back there that this is a tobacco-free facility."

"Is there?" he smiled as he took one last drag and the dropped what was left to the pavement, smashing it into ash with his shoe. "I hadn't noticed."

"Must have been seeing things," I replied as he badged the door open for me. "Good morning, by the way."

"Ugh," he groaned. "I can't wait until the weekend," he said as he led me through the rabbit warren of hallways toward the squad room.

Far bigger than the one in Windeport, it was laid out in a remarkably similar manner, making me suspect even more strongly there was some sort of textbook for the look and feel of police facilities. Cubicles in drab grey stretched in all directions but were lightly filled at that hour; signage hung from the ceiling denoting the various divisions represented, though as we passed through some of them on the way to the sign in the rear for *Robbery/Homicide*, I noted the majority of the cubes were barren.

"Downsizing?" I asked as we rounded a final cube wall.

"For the last four years, yes," he nodded. "The Town Council has this lame-brained idea to offload our less-important work to the County. We don't do any sort of parking enforcement or moving violations these days; no cold cases or financial misconduct."

I raised my eyebrows. "That doesn't leave much."

"Nope," he said, "and fewer people to cover it." He waved to a three-by-six cube that had a phone and cables to connect my MacBook to the network. "Your home away from home."

"Quite likely," I replied, remembering how many late nights I had spent burning the midnight oil in Windeport. As I put my laptop bag on the chair, I turned to Mark. "I need to get my badge, sidearm and ID."

"Chief of the Watch is that way," he said, pointing a lean finger down a side hallway. "She'll set you up. When you get back, we'll go down to records and pull the rest of the evidence for your case."

"Okay," I said, bemused. "I think I have to meet with Chief Andrews, too."

Mark actually laughed. "The old duffer won't be in before eleven. We have time."

"Okay," I repeated, unsure of how to respond to this clear level of disrespect for our commanding officer. Mark didn't seem to mince words, though. "I'll... just go and get my stuff."

"Take your time," he said as he pulled out his pack of cigarettes.

I found the Chief of the Watch behind a bulletproof glass window; she buzzed me through into her little command and control center before pulling her reading glasses down from her frazzled grey mane. "Detective Korsokovach," she muttered as she two-fingered her way across the keyboard of her terminal. Motioning, she had me back up so her web camera could snap a photo, then had me digitally add a signature using a small pad she had to uncover from beneath a stack of paper. Another key press and the printer behind her hummed to life.

"One badge coming up," she said as if we were discussing the weather, turning to the small badge printing machine behind her and grabbing the plastic before it dropped into the bin.

Handing it me, she reached under the desk and pulled out a small gun case, then grabbed another small rectangular box. Cracking open the box revealed my actual badge, and she deliberately entered the number into her computer before opening the gun case and similarly transcribing the serial number into the system. "The Glock was cleaned when it was turned in a few months ago, but I'd recommend giving it a once over. Supplies are down the hall to the right; armory is down the same hall and to the left."

"Thank you," I replied as I accepted the goods.

She waved at me.

The disquiet I'd initially felt upon arrival started to bloom into a significant amount of self-doubt as I pushed back out of the room and into the hallway. I wasn't sure what I'd been expecting; while it certainly wasn't a welcome aboard party, so far, my reception had been lukewarm at best. Trying to stay optimistic, I chalked it up to the differences between a small-town department and a more robust city version.

Back at my desk a short while later, Mark was still absent; strictly speaking, other than his offer to walk me further through the case, I really didn't need him. Setting up my laptop, I logged back in and re-opened the case files once more along with the Word document I had created the night prior. The first entry on my personal notes caught my attention – *schedule interview* -- and I glanced at the clock on the computer's desktop. It wasn't quite eight... would a famous author be up at that hour? Mainers tended to be dawn-to-dusk types, which I knew wasn't exactly the case in California. Taking a chance, I punched up the phone number for Dr. Frankenhoffer from the case files and then picked up my landline.

To my surprise, a melodic female voice answered. "Hello?"

"Dr. Frankenhoffer? This is Detective Korsokovach, Rancho Linda P.D.? I'm sorry to bother you so early on a Monday... is this a good time?"

There was a chuckle at the other end. "I've been up since four-thirty, Detective. I have to be to the pool by five, and it takes longer and longer for these old bones of mine to get moving."

"No kidding," I replied. "Which pool, do you mind me asking?"

"I don't. I swim with the Masters team over at the high school two or three times a week. Why do you ask?"

It was my turn to laugh. "I think we met this morning, then," I said. "I'm the new guy."

"No shit," she said. "You're the one that came with Drew this morning?"

"Yes," I laughed, slightly amazed someone worth (I looked again) close to ten million could be found at the local high school with the common people. "I didn't connect the dots when he introduced me to Rosie."

"Happens all the time. Then again, we're all in swimsuits, goggles and caps. Not likely I looked much like my book jackets."

"True," I smiled into the phone. "Anyway, I've just been assigned your case."

"I figured," she said. "I suppose you want to come talk to me?"

"I do," I said. "I know you're busy – it says on your file we've had trouble connecting---"

"Say what?"

I paused. "Maybe I'm reading this wrong, but the note here from the last detective states you were hard to reach."

There was a moment of silence. "Detective," she said slowly, "other than the book tour I did ten years ago, the only other time I've left Rancho Linda or Orange County was that weekend my poor housekeeper was killed. I'm a writer. I don't as a rule travel; I stay at home doing my research."

"My apologies," I said, a bit perplexed. "When is a good time for me to visit?"

"Can you come after one? I prefer to write in the morning."

"That's perfect, I'll see you then," I replied, replacing the handset.

Staring at the fabric of the cubicle wall in front of me, it felt as though something important had landed in my lap. I wasn't entirely certain what, though; unbidden, Sean popped into my brain, for it was *exactly* the sort of feeling he'd often get – and one that would lead to a critical connection later. Part of it was that I couldn't make sense of the fact that Rosie had been so open to meeting, given what the file (and Mark) had said; the other part was having seen her earlier that morning without realizing she was the suspect in a major crime.

Context is everything, I mused. *And I am missing it at the moment.*

I was so lost in my thoughts it wasn't until he gently started to massage my neck I realized Mark had returned. The forwardness of his touch snapped me back into the here-and-now, and I turned, a little annoyed. "You're back," I observed, trying to shrug him off.

"You're tense," he replied, redoubling his efforts.

"Mark," I said, a note of warning in my voice. "I know I've not finished the HR checklist yet, but I'm pretty sure this could be misconstrued..."

"Jesus, man," Mark nearly growled as his hands snapped away from my shoulders. "Chill."

I swiveled my chair to face him as he leaned against the partition wall, arms crossed. "Let's just get this out in the open," I said. "Yes, I am gay. No, I am not looking for a relationship. No, I will not be hitting on cute guys here at the office. And no," I said, standing up and seeing my six-two form was nearly eye-to-eye with him, "I am not looking for an office romance that is likely barred by regulations." I maintained eye contact with him and saw an odd sort of defiance flaming there. "Any questions?" I asked.

"Damn," he smiled. "You're hot when you get angry."

"I'll take it as an intended compliment," I said neutrally. "Like you, I am a professional. My love life – or yours – belongs outside of this office. And I would appreciate it if you would respect the boundaries that connotes."

"Are you seeing anyone right now?" he asked, a half-smile on his face.

My jaw dropped slightly. "Were you not *listening*?" I asked. "Look, I don't know how to make this any plainer. If I were a woman and you were doing this, we'd already be writing up a complaint for sexual harassment."

Mark leaned down slightly. "Good thing you're not a woman, then," he whispered.

"You're missing the point!" I said, more than a little irritated. "This isn't acceptable behavior, no matter the genders involved. Did you sleep through the mandatory HR session on that?" I crossed my arms. "Even my little department back in Maine made us watch the video. It was pretty clear to me that the rules applied equally."

Mark tried to put a hand on my shoulder, which I neatly side-stepped. Arching an eyebrow, he smiled again. "You are going to be an interesting partner to work with, Vasily."

"Partner?" I asked, thrown by the sudden shift in the conversation. Intellectually I knew he had done it intentionally to divert from the main topic.

"Yes," he smiled wider. "Didn't Andrews tell you? You're my number two."

Eight

"With respect, Mark, my impression was I would have someone assigned to *me*," I said.

I couldn't help the tiny flame of anger that he was clearly treating me as a junior, given his unwelcome overtures to me and lack of candor with respect to the case I was working. Replaying my interview with Chief Andrews, I was certain he had promised me I was getting a Detective Senior Grade gig with all the trimmings: department provided car, nice paycheck and a second to support me – my own version of what I had done for Sean all those years. To have moved coast-to-coast only to land into a nearly identical position to the one I had given up was insane.

"I don't know what to tell you, Detective," Mark said, though his shit-eating grin told me otherwise. "Why don't you finish up your onboarding and then we'll go through the cases you are going to be working on."

"Cases? Plural?" I asked. "Chief Andrews---"

"Doesn't have a fucking clue and, I will remind you, is retiring in less than thirty days. There is real work to be done, and we are, as you can see, shorthanded."

"May I see your badge?" I asked.

"What?"

"Your *badge*, Detective." I held out my hand.

Looking at me askance, he felt around his belt and unclipped his badge, plopping it into my palm.

I held it up as if I were scrutinizing it closely. "Ah, just as I suspected."

"What?"

"It doesn't say you're God," I smiled coldly. "But it does say you are bullshit incarnate," I added as I handed it back to him. Turning, I sat down in my chair. "I have work to do, Detective. If I have time, I'll circle back to you so we can go over the Frankenhoffer case."

I felt Mark shift behind me. "Well played," he laughed. "Catch you on the flip side, dude."

Ignoring his footfalls as he presumably went for yet another smoke, I turned my attention to my laptop and the small number of emails sitting in my brand-new inbox. The one I'd been told to expect from HR was there, and opening it provided me the links to various HR-system pages to finish signing up for my benefits. I snorted at the list of required training classes that needed to be done in the next thirty days, including the aforementioned sexual harassment one.

There was an email from Chief Andrews scheduling me for a noon-time meeting, which made me frown. I'd hoped Mark wasn't right about my new boss having already checked out, but a quick look at the virtual in-and-out board told me the Chief had yet to arrive that day. I paused at the final email; it was from an awfully familiar address, and I let my mouse hover over it nearly a full minute while I was wracked with indecision. Reminding myself of my earlier conversation regarding professionalism, though, I gritted my teeth and opened it.

From: Colbeth, Sean <sean.colbeth@windeport.me.gov>

To: Korsokovach, Vasily <vkorso@rancholinda.pd.ca.gov>

Vas –

Congratulations on your new assignment! It goes without saying that Rancho Linda's gain is our loss, and I've reminded Chief Andrews he owes me big time for letting you go. Not that I would have had a say in the matter either way, of course – you are a damn fine investigator that will raise the bar for everyone you work with. Just like it did for me.

The entire team here misses you and wishes you all the best. Your shoes will be hard to fill.

Stay in touch if you can.

--S

My vision blurred slightly, and I blinked hard several times to clear it. *Damn*, I thought. *Even* now *he treats me with respect, when I essentially treated him like shit and ran away from him – from everything.*

Saving the email to a private folder, I tried to regroup; it was becoming evident the guilt at my actions had begun to weigh me down. That, in turn, made me a little angry for in the end, why *should* I be guilty of anything? I'd fled – *left*, I corrected – for California, and the reasons were my own. In theory I shouldn't feel one way or the other about Sean and how *he* felt... and yet, I did. And I worried whether I'd been too rash in my decision. Staring at my now empty inbox, I tried to convince myself it was a fleeting concern that would pass with time.

Sadly, I knew a lie when I saw one.

Sighing, I put aside my email and dug through the case files once more, making notes in my handheld notebook for my meeting with Frankenhoffer after lunch. Reviewing the file was somewhat mindless but also all-consuming, though I did hear Mark return and leave multiple times as the morning dragged on. Somewhat close to eleven, I was rotating the crime scene photos on the screen of my laptop when the desk phone rang.

"Detective Korsokovach," I said as I picked up the receiver.

"Detective," I heard Chief Andrews voice. "Do you have time to meet now?"

"Of course," I said. "Just tell me how to get to your office."

He chuckled. "I'm along the north end of the pod," he said. "The office with big glass windows looking back into the cubes. It screams 'boss.' You can't miss it."

I stood up and immediately saw the destination on the far side of the cube farm. "On my way."

Clicking off, I grabbed my laptop and crossed the wide floor, once more amazed at how quiet the space was. This close to lunchtime I would have expected it to be buzzing with activity; the lack of it seemed to be further evidence of the budget issues Mark had mentioned. What I found more troubling was a question that had kept popping into my head all morning: if the situation was that dire, why on earth did they hire me on?

The reception pod in front of the Chief's office was vacant and had the air of disuse, so I tactfully knocked at the doorframe behind it. "In here," I heard Andrews say.

He was sitting at a long faux wood conference table in a room built to house it; windows looked out on the street in front of the station on one side, and equally as large windows back into the pod. A massive LED television was tuned to the local all-news station in Los Angeles, the volume muted; on a banquet below it was an old-fashioned drip coffee maker with a half-full pot in residence. As I came around to sit opposite him, I could see the other end of the space had a double door into his private office.

"Chief."

"How are you settling in?" he asked as he sipped from a mug that said *Number One Grandpa*.

"Well," I replied. "I met Detective Freidman on the way in; he's promised to provide any insights he can on the case."

"Ah," Andrews said. "Your new partner."

I paused halfway to my seat. "Excuse me?" I said, trying to keep my expression calm. "Partner?"

"Yeah," he nodded slowly. "Not in the traditional sense, but I need you to work with him on this case. As peers, but with you in the lead."

"I'm not sure that's really necessary, Chief," I said, putting my laptop down. "I mean, I have no qualms about asking for help if I get into something that requires a second set of eyes. But if I recall correctly, you hired me specifically because I could work solo."

"That's still true," he said. "And will be once you close this case. But you've seen the Frankenhoffer file now, right?"

"I've reviewed it extensively, yes," I replied.

"A lot is missing from it."

"A *ton* is missing," I corrected. "I wanted to talk to you about that."

"Detective Freidman is an up-and-coming officer," Andrews said. "But in his haste to climb the ladder, he tends to not be as... thorough... as the department would wish him to be. So far that hasn't hindered his close and conviction rate. Until this case."

I nodded slowly. "You want me to get the rest of the details out of him? Or show him the ropes?"

"Both, frankly," he smiled. "You have as many years in as he does, but your background is far more grounded in careful police work. Mark is good, but could be *better*. I need you to mentor him a bit."

"I don't think I am the right person for that," I said. "Honestly, I've been the number two person on the chart for almost a decade. I've never had to take anyone under my wing before."

"Then it will be a growth experience for the both of you," he smiled. "Now, let's talk about the case."

I flipped open the laptop and then did the same with my notebook. "I've gone through what we have so far," I started. "You're probably already aware that enough time has passed it would likely be unusual for us to recover anything at this point. I have to admit to wondering why you assigned me the case."

"You're partially right," he said. "In normal cases, if we've not found the property within a few days – two weeks at most – it's a good bet it's gone. That's doubly true here in Southern California, given how close we are to the border."

I looked at him closely. "What are you hoping I will find at this point?"

"Honestly?" he asked, shaking his head. "I have a gut feeling, but I don't want to taint your impressions before you've been up to the mansion. You need to see the place, *see* the crime scene."

"I'm headed up there after lunch."

He smiled, nodding as if I had confirmed something. "Good. Then, if I am right about you, we'll chat again tomorrow morning."

Nine

The end of my meeting with Chief Andrews created a natural breaking point in my day; after dropping my laptop back at my desk, I grabbed the duffel bag with my workout gear in it from where I'd stowed it beneath my desk and retraced my route to the rear of the station. On my way in, I'd passed the massive locker room for the officers and civilians, a perk that existed in most public safety departments. I wasn't terribly interested in the free weights or circuit of Nautilus equipment but *did* want to make use of the locker HR had assigned me; since my earliest days in Windeport, I tended to run or swim during my official lunch break, and I wanted to start my new gig off the same way.

The room was deserted owing to it being early still for the lunch crowd – or, perhaps, due to the reduction in staff that seemed to be the dark cloud hovering over the station. It took a moment to locate my locker and punch in the code provided by HR; it was a sizable unit, far bigger than what I'd had back in Windeport, and perhaps bigger than the home lockers at the pool where I'd competed. Unzipping my duffel, I pulled out my tights and compression tank top, wrinkling my nose slightly at the odor reminding me I'd used them once already. Used to disrobing quickly, in just a few minutes I was lacing up my sneakers against the bench running down the center of the aisle before capturing my hair in a more rudimentary ponytail. I finished by tying a Nike-logoed kerchief that doubled as a fashionable sweat band, then slid my iPhone inside the band of my tights as I headed for the exit.

The day had warmed up considerably, though by Maine standards any day in the upper seventies in November would have been considered tropical. As I followed the signs from the station to a fitness path that appeared to run behind the property, I wondered how long it would be before my blood thinned enough that anything *below* eighty would feel chilly. I hoped it would be a while.

I found the path to be a wide, evenly graded pebble base that sloped away from me in either an easterly or westerly direction that was essentially parallel to the rear parking lot for the station. I randomly decided to go east, set my Apple Watch workout and began to ramp up my speed. There were giant trees towering over the path that seemed vaguely evergreen or vaguely not; even after living in Maine for as long as I had, and despite the intrinsic tie to the outdoors that entailed, I'd never bothered to become familiar with what was growing up around me. Trees were trees; in Maine, they were tall and full of leaves or needles. In California, they tended to look like something from a tropical island. These were closer to the Maine variety, and they provided a nice modicum of shade against the bright sunshine, reminding me that I should have snagged my sunglasses when I left the condo that morning.

Californians had a reputation for health and wellness, well represented by the steady traffic I encountered as I worked my way down the path as it wound along a reservoir of some kind. Ducks – which felt entirely out of place – were swimming along the calm surface, and I could see a senior citizen with a fishing pole trying his luck on the opposite shore. Much like the pier at the beach, I had grave doubts about anything caught in such waters. As the trail twisted up and away from the manmade lake, the grade increased enough that I began to feel it in my quads – reminding me I had already put in 5k at the pool earlier.

The burning was a pain I was used to from years of two-a-days and intense sessions in the weight room; I was somewhat proud of the fact that, given my current age, I'd managed to retain the classic V-shape musculature of a competitive swimmer, though the six-pack abs had become something slightly less. One nasty side-effect of my abrupt departure from Maine was forgoing my hard-earned spot in the Winter Regionals in Boston; with luck, I'd work my way back into the West Coast version by the new year.

My watch beeped, indicating I'd passed the two-mile mark. A quick glance told me I was holding to a seven-minute mile, a somewhat relaxed pace for me. That made me smile, for I only slowed down when my thoughts were rambling, or I was more interested in my surroundings than normal. The latter was definitely the case given the landscape I was passing through. The tree-lined path gave way to an orange grove; the delicate scent of fresh fruit filled my nose, and I caught migrant workers up in ladders harvesting the muted orange orbs. Then the grove fell away and for a time I ran parallel to an abandoned track; like much of Southern Cal, even Rancho Linda had once been connected to Los Angeles through the web of interurban streetcars up to the forties. That they had been replaced by the automobile infuriated me to no end.

One final decline and the path abruptly ended at the rear of an In-N-Out burger stand. Feeling like I was seeing a sign from heaven, I stopped my workout and trotted across the lot, wiping as much sweat as I could from my face with the bottom of my muscle tee. As I rounded the outdoor patio dining section, I stopped short.

"Drew?"

Standing at one of the two-top pedestals, Drew had his back to me and therefore hadn't seen my approach. His dark hair, ruffling in the slight breeze, was what had initially caught my attention; as he turned at the sound of his name, I saw he was dressed in a loose-fitting tie-died t-shirt over skinny jeans that looked as though he'd painted them on. The way they hugged his tight ass was hard to ignore and sent an immediate bolt of desire through me.

As his eyes caught mine, I had a high school teenager moment, realizing my interest in him would be plainly visible – and I had no textbook or backpack to hide behind. Drew smiled, then smiled wider when his eyes drifted downward. I tried to casually twist away and cover the worst of it by tugging on the bottom of my shirt, but the damage was done.

"Damn," he said as he swiftly moved over to me, helpfully blocking the view for others on the patio. He was just close enough I could smell the understated cologne he wore. "We can't let *that* go to waste, now can we?"

"It's my lunch hour," I said, surprised at how husky my voice sounded. "I don't have a lot of time. Maybe hold that thought? Until tonight?" I managed to get out.

"There is no way you are showing up like that – all hot and bothered, emphasis on *hot* – only to leave me here to die from terminal tumescence."

"It's only for a few hours," I grinned a bit slyly. "Think of it as motivation."

"Only if you're wearing this outfit when I see you again." He leaned in. "Promise?"

"Cross my heart," I laughed. "Sweat and all. I get off at five."

"I'll grab my beauty rest and see you at seven? I have to be to work at ten."

"Deal."

I grabbed a cheeseburger with onions and a side of fries, then joined him at the table long enough to wolf down the much-needed calories. As I left him – again with promise to see him that evening – I knew we weren't quite to the "kiss goodbye" part of our relationship; I was also keenly aware that I might only be Drew's rather exotic flavor of the week. At the moment, I was okay with what we had going, but harbored no illusions that it could be over in a blink of an eye.

I couldn't help the thoughts of what our evening might look like as I headed back to the station.

Ten

Drew's welcome interruption required me to step up the pace for the run back to the station; I similarly had to dash through the showers so I could get back out on the road to make my appointment with Dr. Frankenhoffer. My long hair was still quite wet when I slid into the SUV and pulled out of the lot; I hoped the darker color of my polo would hide the water stains somewhat, but there was no chance my hair itself would be dry anytime soon.

The mansion was at the very edge of the city limits, and not particularly easy to get to. It was easy to see it had been built back when Rancho Linda was barely a thousand homes; nestled up into the hills that surrounded the valley that was the city, it had to have commanded fabulous views of the ocean. Slightly off putting were the half-dozen active oil pumpjacks that were slowly rising and lowering, attempting to feed the endless energy needs of the economy. As I turned into the tall gate flanked by two bronze lions, I assumed the pumpjacks had come long after the original producer who'd built the mansion had passed on to the great cinema in the sky. It felt like something he would have fought.

Golden-colored pavers comprised the driveway, clicking under the tires of the SUV as I slowly climbed toward the mansion. Snaking around a well-manicured lawn, I was somewhat surprised not to see gardeners clipping away at the hedges running along the edge. I wasn't the least bit surprised to find a tiered fountain inside the circle of pavers at the end of the proverbial yellow brick road; I pulled up in front of the massive steps leading to an extremely oversized portico protecting two mahogany doors intricately carved with a pattern that could have only come straight out of Frank Lloyd Wright's files. Another pair of bronze lions flanked the steps, and as I hiked toward the entrance, I realized everything about the mansion was larger than life, reflective, perhaps, of the industry the original owner had been a part of.

I bypassed the huge knockers shaped in the face of a lion (and wondering what the connection might be with that particular animal) and depressed the doorbell. This close, the mansion felt like it was hulking over me, almost with a physicality that was hard to quantify. As high up as we were, there was extraordinarily little noise coming from the city below us save for a gentle hiss of traffic from the distant freeway. I was unable to hear the bell go off, but a few moments of waiting saw the left door crack open slightly to reveal a young Hispanic woman in a house cleaner outfit.

"Yes?"

"Detective Korsokovach? To see Dr. Frankenhoffer?"

"Of course. If you would follow me? Mistress is waiting for you in the solarium."

No kidding, I thought. *A freaking solarium? Just like that one in the Bogart movie?*

Pulling the door open wider, I followed the young woman into the cool, darkened interior, finding myself in a massive foyer with a classic Hollywood staircase arching up either side to a central landing against the rear wall. A garish chandelier hung down from an ornate fixture, casting gentle light across the terrazzo tile; oddly, the space was bereft of any other ornamentation. There was no furniture, no half-naked statue of a Greek god, no tall oil paintings gracing the whitewashed walls. I'd spent much of my youth with the one-percenters, so I knew they liked their ostentatious display of wealth – if not for them, to wow visitors of the lower castes (of which I was now a part).

Our footsteps echoed as we crossed the space and entered a small hallway beneath the landing for the floor above. This, too, was remarkable in as much as there was nothing notable along the walls, no random coatrack, no potted plant; if I hadn't known better, I would have assumed the house was a foreclosure sale and I was a potential buyer. Reaching an intersection, my guide turned right; the air began to feel more humid, and the familiar scent of chlorine began to permeate everything.

A fogged glass door was at the end of the hallway, and my guide pulled it open, waving me through in a rush of hot, humid air. Stepping across the threshold, I immediately began to sweat, and realized I'd needn't have worried about my wet hair staining my shirt after all.

Flora of all sorts overwhelmed the glassed-in patio-like space. Pushing back tall fronds of something, I followed a weaving path of slab stones to a wider space in the center that was dominated by a decorative swimming pool. An ornamental waterfall cascaded over river rocks at one end, causing ripples to emanate across the surface and give the pool the illusion of movement. Pairs of chairs ringed the pool, each set surrounding a small table with a single orchid within a vase; each was of the same, light purple color. My host was sitting at a small couch on the far side of the pool, flipping through some paper on the coffee table in front of her. The pages of whatever she was reviewing had started to curl under the oppressive humidity.

I unbuttoned my polo a bit, feeling the sweat trickling down my face and beneath the knot of my ponytail; what parts of my hair that had managed to dry on the ride over quickly became as damp as if I'd just stepped out of the shower. The athletic fabric of the shirt was normally quite breathable, but I found it began to stick to me uncomfortably as it was overwhelmed by the combination of my perspiration and the general humidity of the space. Dr. Frankenhoffer, however, was bundled up in a sweater and long pants, and appeared to be sipping on a hot beverage – hot enough the steam was visible even inside the hothouse. She caught my approach over the top of her mug and waved me over.

"Detective!" she cried out as she stood. "Right on time."

I tried to surreptitiously wipe my hand on the back of my khakis before holding it out to her; it was a terrible idea, for it came up damper than ever. Her hand, surprisingly, was dry as a bone, emphasizing the clamminess of my own. "Thanks for meeting with me, Doctor," I said as she gestured me to a seat perpendicular to hers.

"My pleasure, and please, call me Rosie."

"If you'll call me Vasily," I replied as I pulled out my notebook. Much to my dismay, the pages had already grown damp; fortunately, my notes from the office hadn't yet begun to run.

"That's an interesting name. Balkans?" she mused.

"Ukraine, actually. My parents emigrated in the early sixties as kids when the Soviet Union was still in vogue. I'm first generation American."

"Yes," she said, nodding to herself. "I can see that in your chin."

"My… chin?"

"Yes. Very Ukrainian."

"I've never been told that before. Is it a good thing?"

"For Ukrainians, I suppose," she laughed.

I smiled, trying to ignore that it felt as though I were sitting in a puddle of sweat. "Well, if it helps me pick up a date, I'll take it."

"It should." She paused and then added without prompting: "I have a heart condition."

I looked up from my notes. "You do?"

"Yes. Had a pacemaker/defibrillator installed a few years ago; thing zaps me every now and again to make sure I keep a steady rhythm. Can't feel a thing when it happens. Anyway," she sipped at her coffee. "The blood thinners they have me on make me feel cold all the time. This is the *only* room in this entire place where I feel moderately tepid."

I nodded. "I've heard that can happen," I replied, blinking the sting of sweat away. I figured at this rate I had about ten minutes before I was thoroughly dehydrated. "Can't they adjust your dosage?"

"They tried. I gave up and essentially moved into here. Aside from my writing room, the mansion is pretty much empty at this point."

"I couldn't help but notice that on my way in," I said. "It did seem rather empty for a place of this... elegance."

"Kind of you to say," she laughed, and it was a rich, Lauren Bacall-esque sound that filled the solarium. "Once I knew I was pretty much never going to use any of that stuff, I sold it all at a charity auction. Raised six million for the local foodbank."

I tried not to gasp. "Six? *Million*?"

"Yeah," she said with no trace of pretention. "I had a few original oils from notable painters and period furniture from the turn of the last century. None of it was mine, it came with the mansion when I bought it back in the eighties." She leaned over to me. "Did you know he died right there in that pool?"

"The last owner?"

"Yep. He was ninety-eight and very alone at the end. His housekeeper found him face down. Police thought he stumbled in and drowned."

"That's wild," I said, intrigued that the mansion had seen more than its share of death.

"Yeah. What's really wild is the kids didn't want the place after he kicked the bucket. Not even the grandkids. I picked this place up for a song; the real estate agent was practically paying *me* to take it off her hands." She looked at me and laughed again. "You look like you're too young to remember the eighties."

"Guilty as charged," I smiled back.

"God," she smiled, sitting back in her chair, coffee mug pressed to her chest. "Those were the days. My first few books hit it big then, and the market was doing so well my investment manager doubled my money three times over five years. I wanted to make sure I had enough when the books stopped selling, though thankfully that's not happened yet. And," she added, waving at the mansion in general, "this place takes a fair amount of cash for upkeep. Not as much as those castles over in England, but close."

"You could rent out some rooms to tourists," I observed. "I think that's what they've done."

"Nah," she replied. "Not my style. But you're not here to chew the fat. What do you want to know?"

"Is it normal that you only have one copy of your manuscript? In one place?"

Rosie laughed again. "My young friend, it took an incredible act of courage for me to put away my trusty typewriter and start using that newfangled word processor the publisher likes. I'll be honest: I turn it on, I type on it, I turn it off. When I'm done, the publisher sends someone to download the book and take it back for editing."

"It's not on the internet? Connected to cloud storage?"

"You're speaking a foreign language. I don't even have cable." She sighed. "It's just me and my research."

"You hold a Ph.D. in History?"

"Undergrad was at Stanford; graduate degrees are from Berkeley."

My eyes widened. "That's unusual. Most people don't cross like that."

She shrugged. "You go where the talent is," she replied. "Taught twenty-four years at USC as a tenured professor; I still hold a chair but haven't been in a classroom in nearly twenty years." She laughed. "I'm too famous now for them to try and bully me back. Besides, it looks good to have my name on the department stationary."

"Do you have research associates? Anyone that helps with your work?"

"Not any longer," she sighed. "This last book of mine – and it will be my last, I know that now – is complete on the research side; all that's left now is to put the narrative together. My final research fellow was let go some five years ago."

"I checked out your publishing history---"

Rosie laughed. "Two years, on the dot, for a long, long time." She sighed. "For whatever reason, this one hasn't come together as easy as the rest. I don't know if it's the subject matter or the fact my subconscious isn't ready to be done as an author."

Sipping her coffee, she smiled. "It was only my past prowess as a bestseller that has let me get away with ten years of work and nothing to show for it. My publisher is having kittens waiting for this manuscript. And now I have to start over again from scratch."

"Completely?"

"No," she sighed again. "I've got it all up here," she added, tapping her head with finger. "But the second time is never as good as the first, if you know what I mean. Especially since I'm on a tight deadline now."

"No more Mister Nice Publisher?"

"Pretty much. My editor retired last year and was replaced by this twenty-something – no offense, but your generation knows squat about history and could care less about my credentials. She's only interested in what can sell, and that *used* to be my name. If we can get something out there."

I smiled. "I'll take that as a compliment, seeing that I'm not a twenty-something." I flipped some pages in my notebook. "The day you found your housekeeper, you were coming back from being out of town?"

"Like I said on the phone, first time in years," she said. "I needed a break from the book and took a long weekend up the coast."

"Whereabouts?"

"San Luis Obispo-ish," she said. "I have a small beach house up there." Rosie shrugged. "One of the perks of having money to burn, I guess."

"How long were you out of town?"

"Four days; I drove up on a Thursday, stayed the weekend and drove back Sunday morning. I like to beat the traffic if I can, and the Five can be nasty. Got back to Rancho Linda somewhere around one. Came home to find the patio door to my writing room smashed and Lillianna expired on the oriental rug. Helluva way to arrive home."

"How long had---" I looked at my notebook, realizing I'd never gotten the actual *name* of her housekeeper until that moment. "Uh, Lillianna, worked for you?"

"She came with the house," Rosie laughed. "Along with the gardener and chef. They were all here the day that mogul passed away. Lillianna was the last of them, actually," she added softly. "I still have a gardener, a chef and a housekeeper, of course, but they all work for an agency now. Not for me directly."

I did the math and wrote the number down on the now-damp page of my notebook. Wiping my hands again on my khakis, I asked: "Was anyone else at the house that evening?"

"Nope," Rosie replied. "Lillianna was the last servant to live in the house with me. I'm alone these days after seven." She looked away. "This place is kind of big for one person. I've been thinking about downsizing, but not until this damn book is finished. Don't need the distraction."

Flipping my notebook closed, I smiled. "That's all I had, other than a desire to see the space where the theft occurred. If you don't mind?"

"Not at all," she smiled as she looked over my shoulder. Turning, I could see the new housekeeper had quietly appeared out of the shadows. "Lorena, please take the Detective to my writing room? And then show him out."

"Of course, Mistress," she said, curtsying slightly before looking to me. "This way, please."

"A pleasure, Dr. Frankenhoffer," I said as I stood. "I may be back with follow-ups later."

"I'll be here."

I followed Lorena out and back into the cooler interior of the mansion; at the intersection, she continued straight and paused at a pocket door in the wall. Grabbing the handles, she slid the doors apart and stood to one side so I could enter.

As crime scenes went, it was fairly banal – reminding me that murder often occurs where you least expect it. The room felt like it had once been the butler's small but well laid out quarters. Barely bigger than the dorm room I'd had at UEM, it *did* have a nice patio sliding door with a magnificent view down into Rancho Linda, though the patio itself was nothing but a small square of flagstone. Mismatched file cabinets that appeared to have been flea market specials lined two walls, with a generic discount furniture store bookcase crammed to overflowing with material of all sorts on the third. A ridiculously small desk with a massive flat screen monitor sat in the middle of the room, facing the window; the CPU was sitting below the desk, the standby power light on its face flashing slowly.

Papers of all kinds were arrayed in neat stacks around the keyboard and mouse, each with a sticky note and a scribbled message. It was highly organized, looking very much like the sorts of professors' offices I'd been in while an undergrad seeking help. I ran a finger to the keyboard and the screen immediately lit up; unsurprisingly, it didn't have a password and her book was glowing inside the word processor program, cursor blinking on the final sentence she'd been working on. Not the best as cybersecurity went, but then again, we tended to focus on external threats from the internet.

Overall, it was not the sort of space I'd expected from a multimillion-dollar writer.

Stepping to the window, I could just make out one of the lions gracing the steps to the front door. "What *is* it with those lions?" I asked my reflection.

"They are the symbol of the company the prior owner ran," Lorena answered from behind me. "Heart of a Lion Productions."

I turned. "I've never heard of it."

She shrugged. "All I know is what the agency told me. That, and the fact that Mr. Andrews had died here, so I wouldn't freak out the first time I saw the pool."

"Andrews?" I repeated, the name snagging at something.

"Yes," she replied as we started back toward the front door. "Thomas Andrews. My understanding is that his family still lives in Rancho Linda."

"I imagine they do," I said thoughtfully. "And I think I know how to find out."

Eleven

When I pulled my running gear back out of my duffel bag much later that evening, it was still damp from my run at noontime, and smelled, if possible, *worse* than before. Grimacing slightly as I pulled the clammy tights on, I reminded myself a promise was a promise; it was a harder case to make when the muscle tank top clung to my skin as though I'd poured a bottle of water over me.

Tying the kerchief back around my head and flipping my ponytail over the knot from the fabric, I turned in the mirror of my bath and wondered if this counted as some sort of cosplay, if roleplaying the part of sweaty jogger was truly going to turn Drew on. I smiled at my reflection, for something *like* that had been an aphrodisiac for a guy I'd dated at UEM; he used to become a quivering mass of excitement if I showed up in his dorm room wearing nylon wind pants, though I'd never fully understood why.

I opted not to slide my iPhone into the damp waistband and instead wandered out into my kitchen, placing it on the counter. Drew wasn't due quite yet, so I had time to wash up my dishes from dinner and ruminate on my afternoon. Inexplicably, Mark had been missing from the station when I'd returned from my interview with Dr. Frankenhoffer; Chief Andrews had similarly been MIA, though when I checked his calendar, he was ostensibly at the City Manager's office for the afternoon. Mark didn't seem all that keen to keep a calendar, and to be honest, despite wanting to ask him some more detailed questions about the case, I truly didn't want to interact with him any more than was necessary.

One question proved easy to answer, though. The Rancho Linda Public Library and historical archives was just down the block, and a short walk there ended with me getting to know the reference librarian a little better.

"Thomas Andrews?" she'd said with a half-smile. "He's practically considered a founding father of Rancho Linda. That mansion of his was built during his heyday as a producer."

"I understood that when he passed, no member of the family wanted the house?" I'd asked.

"No," she'd replied. "Chief Andrews' father refused, literally walking away once the estate had been settled. They took the money, though; as I understand it, Thomas Andrews indirectly wound up putting his great-grandkids through USC."

Drying my plate at the sink, I wondered why the Chief hadn't disclosed he was tangentially related to the case, though even I had to admit it was a tenuous connection at best. Still, it bothered me a bit that he'd not told me his grandfather had apparently been the owner of the mansion; it was a nagging loose end, and I hated loose ends with a passion.

I'd already gone through the case files earlier, and knew the items stolen from the mansion had yet to make an appearance at any of the usual places in the county. Still, I took an hour to call around to multiple pawn shops and at least two eBay storefronts just to be complete. None had anything matching the list I was looking at, but all promised to call me the moment something flagged came in. Though I'd taken them at their word, I doubted strongly I would hear from them.

Glancing down to the paperwork on my counter, I could see the desktop that had been stolen was fairly old; that meant the resale value would be relatively low, even on the black market. Putting my hands on the counter, I shook my head, for it, too, felt like an oddball loose end. The flat screen television I understood; a desktop running an out-of-date operating system and was unable to connect to the internet was a second loose end. Picking up my wineglass, I sipped the chardonnay I'd picked up at Trader Joes on my way home, wondering.

Why the computer?

Swirling the wine around thoughtfully, I shifted the paper and saw my approved travel form. Even without the Chief being present, I'd been able to push through a request to drive up to San Luis Obispo in the morning to check on Dr. Frankenhoffer's story. Mark had taken it at face value, and while it rang true to my ears as well, a nagging doubt in the back of my head required me to make the trip. I frowned slightly at the Comfort Inn Travel had booked me into – I was a bit of a snob when it came to hotels, as Sean's preference for the Marriott brand had rubbed off on me – but I was forced to live within the per diem of my new department.

Sean.

Dammit! I mentally yelled at myself as I put the glass on the counter. *Just when I think I can get through a day without you, you appear.*

I uncorked the bottle and poured another healthy helping of wine into the glass, even though the rational part of my brain was nearly screaming it might be best to keep my wits about me with a guest arriving. Downing half the glass, I refilled it again, telling myself that I didn't care.

The cork was just going back in when my phone buzzed with the number from the front door. Assuming it was Drew, I put it on speaker. "Hey gorgeous, you're early."

"Vasily? Do you have a minute?"

My fuzzy brain registered that it wasn't Drew's voice. "Who is this?"

"It's Mark. Detective Freidman?"

"I'm a little busy, Detective," I replied, somewhat horrified that he'd tracked down the location of my condo. I was sure the information was in the HR system, of course, but etiquette and policy kept it private unless it was shared intentionally. "Can it wait until the morning?"

"I wanted to talk about the case. The, uh, Franken—Franke—Frankenhoffer? Case?"

As full of cotton as my brain was – three glasses of wine will do that to a guy, even one with as much muscle as I have – it was easy to tell that Mark, himself, was slightly drunk. I wondered what it meant that the two of us were in that state on a Monday, no less. "This really isn't the best time," I said.

"Ten minutes."

While I did have questions for him, I didn't like the fact he was here. In my home. Glancing at the clock in my phone, I knew it was technically possible to get him in and out before Drew arrived and I *truly* got down to business. "Fine. Five minutes."

"Okay."

Feeling like I was making the wrong decision, I nonetheless buzzed him in and waited by the kitchen counter for the knock on my door. "This had better be good," I said as I swung it open, only to stop and stare at him, stupefied.

Mark was wearing a snug muscle t-shirt that exposed his massive biceps and hugged an extremely well defined six pack; he had a pair of microfiber shorts on over compression leggings, with carefully matched sneakers. His normally perfectly coiffed hair was sticking up in all the wrong places. Holding his phone and wallet in one hand, he had his sunglasses in the other; I tried not to stare at the small diamond studs that had appeared on his ears, nor the brilliantly done tattoo of an eagle on his arm.

"I see we were both working out tonight," he said with a disarming smile.

"When did you get piercings?" I blurted, unable to stop my curiosity.

"I don't wear anything at the office," he said as he stepped inside. "Unlike some people, I don't like to advertise."

"I don't advertise!" I said defensively, wondering why I felt it necessary to say anything.

Walking past me, I wondered if it was just the wine that had my pulse pounding in my ears. This version of Mark was almost intoxicating, bearing no resemblance to the boorish one that had been coming on to me earlier. The tiny functioning part of my brain that was left coolly informed me Mark knew exactly what he was doing, that he had correctly guessed I had a weakness for carefully tended to physiques. As the door to my condo glided shut behind me, I could see the gentle curve of his ass sliding beneath the microfiber shorts and decided he'd checked that box rather perfectly.

"The case?" I managed to get out as I walked with some difficulty back to the counter. Fortunately, it was between the two of us. "What did you want to talk about?"

Mark turned those green eyes on mine, and I felt something start to give way. Intellectually, I knew he hadn't come to discuss *anything*, and that what he was truly after was something I wanted no part of providing. But whether it was the wine, or the fact that I desperately needed to get Sean off of my mind, I suddenly didn't care. Before I knew what I was doing, I had rounded the corner of my counter and pulled him to me.

We were of a height, so his lips met mine at nearly the perfect angle. He tasted of tequila, cigarettes and salt, and as he went to my neck, I could smell his expensive cologne co-mingling with the pungent yet somehow virile odor of his recent workout. Slipping a hand under his shirt, I ran it over his rock-hard abs and up to a nipple, tweaking it slightly and eliciting a gasp.

Reaching downward, I found other parts of him were equally as solid, straining against the fabric of his leggings. As I pulled him to the relative softness of the carpeted living room, I decided the case could wait for a bit, carefully ignoring all of the warnings my brain was screaming at me in all caps with respect to fraternization with a fellow officer. For once, my thoughts were focused solely on the moment – and my own personal needs.

It was a mistake I would live to regret.

Twelve

The alarm on my Apple Watch sang out and I dragged myself up from the depths of sleep. We were in the bedroom suite, curled into each other upon the comforter I'd bought for the bed that had yet to arrive; Mark's strong arm was wrapped over me protectively, and his chin was nestled into my shoulder. It was unusual for me to be the one on the bottom, but it was just luck of the draw – as it turns out, we were each used to being the dominant partner, and through an unspoken agreement had swapped back and forth all night.

When we'd finally collapsed into each other, exhausted, I dozed off in his arms much as I'd awoken. Snuggling into him, I felt him adjust slightly and wondered just what the hell sort of mess I had gotten myself into. Looking at my watch again, I sighed and pulled myself out from beneath him, awakening him further.

"What time is it?" he asked groggily.

"Four-thirty."

Mark swore. "What the fuck. Get back down here."

I laughed, though his tone had more than a little ring of command to it. "Sorry, I've got to get to practice."

"Practice? At *this* hour?" he groaned.

"You go when you have the pool," I reminded him as I grabbed my phone and used the flashlight to scrounge for a swimsuit and my sweats. Belatedly I realized I had two missed calls and six text messages; a bolt of guilt shot through me when I realized *who* they were from. "Shit," I breathed as I unlocked the phone and quickly scanned the texts.

"What?"

"Nothing," I said as I hurriedly yanked the briefs up and slid into my sweats. "I've got to run. And you've got to go."

"Fine," he moaned, before turning his megawatt smile on me. "But only if you agree to dinner."

"I remind you that normally it's dinner *first*, sex second," I laughed. "So you owe me two meals."

"I'm good for it," he smiled as I dropped to my knees.

Holding his face in my hand, I kissed him and pulled back. "I hope to God we know what we're doing."

"It's never stopped me before," he said as he gathered his workout clothes and started to pull them on.

"That doesn't surprise me in the least," I said as I grabbed my swim kit and propelled him out the door of my condo.

The entire ride over to the pool, I tried to figure out what to say to Drew. I felt like shit for standing him up, but between the wine and the animal desire that had carried me away, I'd completely lost track of the original plan for the evening. His text messages had gotten progressively more concerned, ending around midnight. Pulling into the lot at the pool, I realized he wouldn't be there since he was only off on Mondays and Wednesdays. That presented a bit of a conundrum as the SUV idled in the parking spot: do I swim, and then try and catch him after practice? Or go directly to the diner and face the music?

As I sat there, immersed in my thoughts, a time capsule from the nineteen-eighties pulled in beside me. It had been years since I'd seen one of those cookie-cutter Oldsmobile Cutlass Calais on the road and not in a movie or television show I'd streamed from that period. This one appeared to be in mint condition, which became less of a surprise when I saw who was behind the wheel.

Rosie put the car into park and got out, then slowly ambled toward the gate; I realized beneath the swim cap and goggles, she looked very ordinary and not anything like a millionaire author. Wrapped in warm sweats, she still looked cold to me. Decision made, I slid out of the SUV and caught up with her.

"Hey," I said. "How are you this morning?"

"Detective!" she smiled. "Well, thank you. After you left yesterday, I managed to bang out two chapters. It's the most I've done in weeks. Apparently, I needed an attractive distraction to get back on course."

I felt my cheeks flame slightly. "Glad to help," I said as we entered the pool deck. "But it wasn't my intent to interrupt you."

"Oh, I don't mind."

"I meant to ask you yesterday – the file I have says you were unavailable for interviews, which is why there wasn't any follow-up before I visited you yesterday. I have a feeling that is in error..."

"No shit. I've been home continuously since the theft and murder of my housekeeper trying to rewrite the missing book. Where else would I be?"

"My thoughts exactly," I nodded as we dropped our gear to the deck and I pulled off my sweatshirt. It wasn't lost on me that her eyes snapped to my abs. "But you *did* talk to Detective Freidman?" I asked as I kicked off the sweatpants.

"Who?"

"Mark Freidman. He was the lead on the case," I explained as I tucked my ponytail into my rubber swim cap.

"No," she said as she slowly unzipped her jacket. "It was a patrolman, Geoff something." She looked at me, a bit confused. "You are the first detective I've spoken to, Vasily."

"Lovely," I said as that dread in my stomach reappeared.

I wound up so lost in my thoughts about the case that I managed to squeeze in an extra thousand meters during practice, then toweled off as quickly as I could before throwing on my sweats and speeding over to the diner. As I'd hoped, I slid into my usual booth just as Drew was coming off shift; he joined me, though his look held more than a little concern.

"Before you say anything," I started, "this one is on me. Something came up and I lost all track of time. I was a lousy friend and didn't text you the moment I knew my evening was going off-script."

"You had me a little worried," he said. "When you didn't buzz me through and then didn't answer--"

"I know, and I'm terribly sorry," I said, reaching across to hold his hand. A tiny part of me was a bit nauseated that, while I wasn't exactly lying, I wasn't being completely forthright with him, either. As an investigator, I was well aware it was the exact kind of prevarication that led to deeper, uglier, costlier consequences later. "This case I have is proving more complicated than it initially appeared."

"Nothing like jumping in at the deep end," he smiled slightly, somewhat mollified. But I could still see the concern on his face, intermingled with a bit of dismay.

"I'd like to make it up to you," I said. "Are you free on Wednesday night?"

"Yeah..." he said, looking away for a moment. "About that," he said as he pulled his hands from mine.

"Uh oh," I said, my stomach roiling further.

"I would have told you last night, under more pleasant circumstances." He looked back at me. "My boyfriend is back in town; he's on leave for ten days, and I'm going to take off with him to spend a bit of it up in Malibu."

I tried to keep the shock from my face. "I know we aren't dating, exactly," I said, trying and failing to ignore my own hypocrisy, "but you could have told me that up front. I'm not one to horn in on someone else's turf."

"You weren't -- *aren't*," he corrected. "We have a rather open definition of 'relationship.' I know he's got guys on the carrier, and he knows

I have... others... here in California. Like you. Casual relationships to get us through."

"*Casual*?" I felt my face flame and eyebrows drop. "I guess I read a bit more into what was going on than I realized."

He saw my expression. "Not like *that*," he corrected. "Casual only in the sense that while I value you and... want you, desperately," he said, lowering his voice, "at the end of the day, I'm committed to him for the long run."

My thoughts were in turmoil and saw no small amount of irony that I was upset at being his backup lover given how I'd spent the prior evening myself. It felt safest to just nod and try to breathe. "When will you be back?" I managed to ask somewhat pleasantly.

"You're okay with this?" he asked instead.

"This is... new for me," I replied honestly. "I tend to be a one-guy-at-a-time dude. Sharing is not in my playbook."

"In fairness, this will never be more than friends-with-benefits. I think we both know that."

I nodded. "Yes," I replied before making a point of looking at my watch. "I've got to go," I said lamely. "I need to get to the office a bit earlier than normal and haven't had a chance to shower."

"You're angry," Drew said.

"Maybe a little," I smiled slightly, "but I have no right to be. Which makes me angrier."

This time, it was Drew that reached for my hand. "I still want to be a friend. *Your* friend."

"I'll need some time to digest my place in the world," I replied. "I'll see you when you get back to Rancho Linda," I added as I slipped out of the booth and fled the diner.

Thirteen

I'd barely been in California five days and had already slept with three different guys; of those, one I'd never see again, one had me in his backup bullpen, and the third represented the most forbidden form of romance my field knew. Clearly, the West Coast had not been a good influence on me. Whatever change I thought moving would provide, this was *not* it.

What the *hell* was wrong with me?

It was a refrain that kept circling my thoughts as I showered and donned more professional clothes for the day. I had no right to be upset with Drew – he'd been more or less honest with me from the beginning, save for having a boyfriend already. I did have cause for concern with Mark, for department regulations tended to be pretty clear about relationships. Fortunately, neither one of us was a superior to the other, which didn't make it any more permissible; it just made it a lesser offense.

Pulling out my trusty duffel, I started tossing items in for my overnight trip to San Luis Obispo. As I dug out a clean pair of tights and a tank-top from a run I'd done at Disney World the prior year, I chuckled at the irony. That I was telling myself there were lesser degrees of "bad" seemed like I had sunk to an all-time low in the morality department – especially for someone in the enforcement profession. So much for setting an example to my fellow citizens.

Skipping breakfast had been an unwise move, especially after working out; I felt the first pangs of a headache warning me that some sustenance beyond the cup of coffee I'd downed prior to storming out of the diner was necessary if I had *any* hope of being remotely human for the day. I'd already located a Starbucks that was along the route to the station but didn't especially feel like one of their fresh-from-a-bag pastries would do the trick. Vaguely remembering some sort of combination bookstore and café at the mall where I'd gathered my first round of apartment necessities, I changed lanes in the early morning traffic in order to turn into the massive but still empty parking lot for the Rancho Linda Mall.

A small gaggle of vehicles were parked close to the entrance, and I slid the SUV into an open spot beside them. Locking it up, I crossed the pavement to the massive set of glass doors and pulled one open; the blast of air conditioning, cranked to full even in late November, attempted to push me back but I persevered. Like most malls, the corridor I found myself in twisted away at an odd angle to the entrance, with retail stores on either side. At that early hour, all of them appeared to be closed to the public, though I could see the occasional head of a staff member bobbing among aisles of product.

Coming around the corner, a food court stretched off in one direction, and seemed to be doing a relatively brisk business. A number of the tables were full, mostly with grey-haired senior citizens. I wondered how many of them had been hiking the interior perimeter of the mall as part of their morning exercise; most of the people I passed were attired in workout clothes from another era, potentially confirming my hypothesis. The rather serpentine layout of the interior of the mall meant my destination was ultimately much further away from the entrance than I would have thought possible; ultimately, though, the amazingly rich fragrance of freshly ground coffee led me unerringly to the wide-open entrance that stood as a welcome beacon to those of us who were part of the Cult of Caffeine.

Entering *The Alternative Way* felt a bit like donning a well-worn favorite pair of jeans; the tastefully laid out floorplan had four-foot-high bookcases arranged in clusters by topic, with plenty of space set aside for comfortable looking reading chairs and couches. One entire wall appeared to have a copy of every major national and international newspaper, with a slightly smaller companion wall holding magazines of all stripes and varieties. The lighting was low, but not dark enough to prevent careful perusing, and was accompanied by a marvelously complementary background soundtrack of contemporary jazz. Two cash registers were contained within an oval desk at the center of the space, and off in the corner was the small café producing the mouth-watering aromatic smells. A switchback bank queue with stanchions held a number of people; glancing at my watch, I wasn't sure if I had as much time as I might need to get through the line, and hesitated.

That attracted the attention of a plump woman with shockingly purple hair who had been curling up some sort of cord in what appeared to be a small performance area. She caught my eye and set the cable down to make her way through the patrons toward me.

"It moves fast," she said, nodding to the line for the barista. "Gertrude is amazing. Unless, of course, you order some sort of triple-shot-of-soy-hold-the-foam misery; then you'll likely wait an hour."

"Good to know," I laughed. "I saw the place this weekend but didn't have a chance to stop in before now."

"Best coffee in town," the woman said, her wide smile warm and friendly. This close, I could see she had on tiny earrings shaped like books. "You must be new to the area."

"I am, kind of," I replied. "I grew up in SoCal, but just recently moved back from the East Coast."

"Job bring you back?" she asked.

"Something like that," I nodded. "It's funny what has changed," I continued, before thinking of my parents. "And what hasn't."

"That, my friend, is the dichotomy that is California." She held out her hand. "I'm Anne," she continued. "Co-owner of the place."

I shook her hand, slightly amazed at how firm her grip was. "Vasily," I replied. "Nice to meet you."

"Same," she smiled, then considered me for a moment. "Given that classical V-shaped body of yours, I'm gonna go out on a limb and say you're the *same* Vasily that competed in the '08 Olympics."

"That's me," I laughed. "You're pretty observant. And seem to have an amazing grasp of ancient history."

"Not so ancient," she chuckled. "Rosie told me a former Olympian had joined the swim team. I wondered if you'd find your way to us."

"You know Rosie?"

"Who doesn't?" she rolled her eyes. "But she's been amazingly generous with both her time *and* her giving, helping us with some of our pet projects." She nodded toward a small unprepossessing table against a far wall. "I lost track of how many weekends she's spent doing book signings as a way to raise funds for our local chapter of the Southern California HIV/AIDS Foundation."

"That's impressive."

"We're quite thankful," Anne replied. "Next month, she's helping us with a readathon to support our Youth LGBTQ outreach." Her smile faded slightly. "Orange County is one of the few areas in the state that, on the whole, seems to be less supportive of kids exploring their identity. We've been trying to change that for the past twenty years, but it's slow going."

"The OC is nothing if not consistent."

"I wish it weren't so true, but there it is."

Something occurred to me as we stood there together. "I have to say, I appreciate you *not* saying 'hey, you were the gay swimmer in '08' when you first introduced yourself to me."

"I take it you hear that a lot."

"More than I care to, even in today's more enlightened era."

"Take heart, Vasily," Anne smiled. "Effective change must be incremental if it's to last; it can be frustrating to see how slow it happens, but it *is* happening."

"You are far, far more optimistic that I am."

Anne shrugged. "My parents came of age during the Sixties and passed down a general 'the world is unfolding as it should' mentality to their kids. I also believe passionately in what my partner and I are doing here, so there's that, too."

The stout woman's outlook on life in general was infectious, and I found myself smiling in response to her smile. "I'm pleased to have met you, Anne. I have a feeling I'm about to become a regular."

"Good," she laughed. "Then I'll make my quota for the week. Come on over here and I'll walk you through the menu," she said as she took me by the arm and propelled me toward the queue; she wasn't kidding, for the line did appear to be moving. "Then you can tell me more about what it's like to be an Olympic Swimmer."

"As much as I would love to do that, I have to get to work," I said sadly.

"I figured," she replied. "Maybe we can get you back on a weekend. I have a feeling some of the younger members of our youth group would appreciate hearing how you handled being out on the world stage."

"I'm not exactly a role model," I hedged, given how many men I had churned through in just the last five days.

"Aren't you?" she smiled. "Come, even if you don't think you are. You might be surprised."

I wanted to say no, but her expression was so genuine, I found myself nodding. "All right. Let me send you a few dates and we'll work something out. Do you have a card or something?"

"Just call the number on your receipt," she laughed. "We're here, like, all the time."

FOURTEEN

The massive squad room was just as empty as before, a status I now knew didn't change more than a few degrees during the day. Sipping my second macchiato from *The Alternative Way*, I logged into my laptop and pulled up the department policies I was most concerned with violating. I'd made it through most of them when I heard footsteps heading in my direction.

Looking up, I watched as Mark rounded the corner wearing that shit-eating grin of his and carrying coffee from Dunkin. "Hey," he said as he leaned up against my desk. "How was the pool?" he asked. "I've been fantasizing about you in those briefs you put on, by the way."

"*Dude*," I hissed, eyes darting to see if anyone had overheard him. "Not appropriate for the office!"

"If you hadn't noticed, we're almost the entire division right here," he replied. "The guys on swing shift are never here in the daytime, and it's at least ten rows of empty cubes before you hit the property detectives." He sipped again. "No one is paying attention to us. Trust me."

I stood up and got close enough I could lower my voice. "Mark, whatever this thing is between us, we need to disclose it to the Chief. Regulations are pretty clear--"

"He won't care," Mark said.

"We're *colleagues,*" I emphasized. "This could impact our working relationship."

"We're adults," he replied. "Aren't we?"

"That's not my point," I countered. "We have to do this by the book. If something goes wrong---"

"God," he breathed. I was close enough to him I could smell the cream from his coffee on his breath. "You are sexy when you get righteous."

I shook my head as I stepped away, crossing my arms. "This is going to be trouble," I observed.

"We'll see," Mark said. "I've got to roll to a scene."

"New case?"

"Yeah, probably nothing major. Homeless guy washed up in the arroyo behind a strip mall. I'll have it wrapped by lunch. You?"

"I'll be out for a day; I have to drive up to San Luis Obispo."

"You're... what?" he said. "Will you be back? I had dinner all planned out."

"Not until tomorrow night," I said. "Sorry - I completely forgot until just now."

"Why are you going up?" he asked casually.

"Just being thorough," I replied wondering why he was interested and knowing it was a move *he* should have done while he was the lead on the case.

"Good luck, then," he said as he turned and headed for the lot.

I watched his (admittedly) cute ass as it moved away from me, and then caught Chief Andrews as he crossed in front of Mark. Dashing from my pod, I caught him a few rows from his office. "Chief? Got a minute?"

He smiled. "I've got ten. Then I am in yet *another* transition meeting."

I followed him into the conference room and stood behind one of the high-backed chairs as he put his briefcase into his office and then returned. "How did the interview go?"

"Well," I said. "I'm reasonably certain now there *was* no robbery; I think it's a cover for the missing desktop computer. If I'm right, it's not missing at all, just, shall we say, misplaced for the moment."

Andrews nodded. "Good. Why?"

"I think Dr. Frankenhoffer is reluctant to stop writing; I'm not sure why, yet, but I think she's being pressured to retire. I need to get ahold of her contract with the publisher, but my conversation with her yesterday makes me think she's out of step with her editor and what they think will sell. The missing computer extends how much longer she'd be, essentially, on the books for the publisher. Once that book goes out, I think they'll cut her loose." I shrugged. "I need to see the contracts. I'm fairly sure she'll let me, but I want some leverage first."

Andrews nodded again, and smiled. "And the murder?"

It was my turn to return the smile. "I understand now why you want this case reviewed. But it would have been best had you told me you were related to the former owner of the mansion."

"Damn," he nodded again. "Sean was right. You *are* good."

"I just connected the dots," I said. "Detective Freidman might have, but I think he was distracted for some reason."

"Story of his life." The Chief turned to the window. "My family has never believed that Grandpa 'slipped' and drowned in that pool," he said. "But the servants stuck to that story right to the end; as a detective myself, I tried to poke around the details, but they wouldn't talk. As they got older, I grew hopeful, but nothing came of my efforts."

He turned back to me. "Secrets, though, have a way of finding the daylight," he said as he walked back to his office. Opening up his briefcase, he withdrew a small envelope and walked it back to me. Handing it over, he said, simply, "Read this."

It was a plain envelope, hand addressed to the Chief; flipping it over, I could see it came from the mansion. Pulling out the small half-folded letter, I unfurled it and saw it was from the housekeeper and dated three days before her death.

Chief -

I've lived with this for as long as I can stand it. Now that I am the last left of the original staff, and given my age, I think it's time for me to come out of the cold. I'll tell you what I know, and finally give you the peace you and your family deserve.

Mistress is out of town for a few days. Please visit the mansion when you receive this.

-- Lillianna Toshiyuka

I looked at Chief Andrews. "What did she say?"

"I have no idea," he said sadly. "This came while I was out of town myself. The timing, though, is more troubling: if, as you suspect, Dr. Frankenhoffer staged the theft of her computer, someone else knew she would be out of town that same weekend – and Lillianna would be alone."

My eyes flicked back to the letter. "This possible murder was more than thirty years ago, Chief. Whatever she had to say wouldn't have been remotely useful in court."

"The law is not always what people are afraid of, Detective. You should know that."

I nodded. "True. Absolutely true." I re-folded the paper and slid it into the envelope. "You want me on this case, too?"

"Most definitely. Check in with me regularly, but for propriety's sake, keep me out of the investigation."

I blanched slightly at the word *propriety*, and he caught it.

"Everything okay?" he asked. "Have you worked out your relationship with Detective Freidman?"

"We have indeed," I said, trying hard to keep the irony from showing in my face.

"Good," he replied, eyeing me thoughtfully. "If you'll permit me to impart some advice? Be careful with that one, Detective. He's a handful."

"I will keep that in mind, Chief," I said as I bowed out of the conference room.

Fifteen

It quickly became clear I'd not regained that unique understanding of traffic all true road warriors in California sported, for I badly misjudged rush hour and got caught crawling through downtown Los Angeles. None of the routes my iPhone recommended shaved more than a few minutes off the total time, so I gritted my teeth and slowly slogged my way through the skyscrapers and overpasses, suddenly nostalgic for the backroads of Maine. The concrete jungle wasn't very appealing in the midday sunshine, and as the temperatures rose, I could see the tempers of my fellow drivers were similarly flaring.

The mess that was Los Angeles put me an hour behind schedule, but I made up a little of it after clearing Thousand Oaks; it was a weekday, so traffic was light heading north on the 101. The coastal drive wasn't unlike Route One in Maine, actually, and to be honest, I enjoyed paralleling the ocean for a few hours. The only thing better would have been having had the department issue me a sporty unmarked convertible. The drive reminded me of cases I'd had in far flung parts of Maine, when Sean and I had been brought in to resolve a thorny case the locals couldn't handle – or which was more common, to *be* the local cops because the town was too small to support a department of its own. I'd made more than a few trips to The County with him, and even then, could recall the smell of freshly cooked potato chips from the factories that hugged the acres of farms.

And there he was *again*.

Rounding a curve that hugged the rugged hills overlooking a part of the California coast, Sean had popped into my thoughts, unbidden. It almost felt like in my unguarded moments, memories of him would pounce, reminding me of what I had left behind. Not even my rather steamy evening with Mark had erased my brain's ability to recall him sitting beside me, musing on the case at hand, his dirty blonde curls shifting as he spoke. Sean had always been a supreme source of confidence for me to draw upon, and I wondered if my current wallowing in self-doubt had contributed greatly to his appearance.

That made me smile, to think I'd crafted a virtual Yoda to nudge me back onto the straight-and-narrow. I wondered if it meant something that I was self-aware enough at some level to know I was entering uncharted, and possibly dangerous territory – that having Sean standing by as some sort of virtue totem was both a warning and a reminder of who I was, or who I wanted to be. *Needed* to be.

Trying to push Sean – and, to a lesser extent, Mark – from my thoughts, I started sorting through my plan when I arrived upstate. A quick property record search had given me the cottage Rosie owned, which technically was outside of San Luis Obispo and instead in a small oceanfront village named Saint Lucie, a spot that, according to the Chamber of Commerce website, specialized in "sunsets, true Italian gelato, and a general sense of wellbeing." It had sounded like a realized version of Lake Woebegone, making me somewhat intrigued to see if everyone was truly above average.

My hotel was ostensibly in the "heart" of the village, nestled up into the hills overlooking the rocky shoreline. From Apple Maps, it looked like their version of Main Street lasted exactly one block, making me wonder how they hosted tourists at all. That same Chamber page had listed one church (non-denominational), one bank, a post office, a single bar and a small grocery store. I was betting getting together enough townsfolk for a night of Bridge was pretty difficult.

I stopped for a late lunch in Santa Maria, just south of my destination. Bypassing the McDonald's initially, I hunted for something heathier. Sadly, I spied an Olive Garden, and couldn't resist the temptation of their salad and breadsticks. Finding a spot in the lot, I locked the SUV and entered; the lunch crowd was in its last throes, so I easily found a table and was happily considering whether to have the lasagna (an all-time favorite) or something more sensible like the shrimp fettuccini. It was a tough choice, one that was shattered when my phone buzzed.

Turning it upward, I saw the Maine prefix and groaned. I knew eventually I would need to actually talk to him, if for no other reason than to let him know I was alive and well. But not yet. Not that day. I silenced the buzzing and flipped it around again, though not without repercussions. My stomach suddenly felt like it was roiling, so I changed course and stuck with the unlimited soup, salad and breadsticks lunch special. Carbs had a way of calming my stomach and my mental angst. But only when paired with a long workout, which I'd hoped to get in that evening.

The romance of the road had soured by the time I returned to the SUV; arriving in Saint Lucie, I drove past my hotel and the six buildings that were the entirety of Main Street, continuing northward a mile until I located the turnoff I needed. As the unimproved dirt road wound its way through the thick forest, branches shot off at regular intervals to the smaller properties that were along it; Rosie's spot had pride of place, the only lot fronting the shoreline proper. Given what she had paid for the spot, I had assumed it would have a magnificent view; as I pulled up to the cottage, I wasn't disappointed in the least.

Not being a student of architecture, I had no idea what style the place was other than it looked like something from what I knew as the "arts and crafts" movement of the nineteen-forties. It felt squat but had a steep roofline that bespoke a generous interior of at least two floors; sided with cedar shake panels, it was painted brown with green trim, and recently done, too. A brick chimney rose at one end, and windows were everywhere. There was a wraparound wood porch that started at the steps below which I'd parked the car; wanting to confirm a hunch, I exited the SUV and climbed the short set of treads, then wandered around the U-shape to the ocean-facing side of the cottage. As I expected, the far wider section running along that side hung precariously over the edge of the cliff the cottage seemed to be hugging. I wasn't entirely sure how comfortable I would feel lounging in the jacuzzi I discovered, but then again, the view was quite spectacular; I supposed after steeping like tea in the boiling water, you might be lulled into a false sense of security. Leaning over the wooden railing and seeing the surf crashing on the rocks far below, I decided it would take more than a soak in the hot tub to make me comfortable – like an entire six pack of Samuel Adams, maybe. Or two.

Stepping back from the railing, I wondered what her earthquake insurance premium might be. I suspected it was many, *many* multiples more than my annual salary. The sun was low in the horizon, but I knew I still had a good two hours of daylight left. Where to begin, however, was another matter entirely, but even so I was reasonably sure it would be enough time to find what I hoped would be there.

It seemed logical to start at the front of the house, so I circled back to where I'd parked the SUV. Peering through the tall window by the quaint front door, I could see a large space that ran front-to-back. I was staring into the sun, so I retraced my steps around the porch and found myself in front of massive sheets of glass, more modern than the rest of the house; stretching up to the second story, I was sure it gave the interior unobstructed views of the ocean. Trying not to leave fingerprints, I nonetheless pressed my face to the window and could clearly see furniture covered in white dust covers, vaguely arranged as if they were a couch and two easy chairs; another set of humps faced the fireplace. An open-plan kitchen was tucked into the far corner, just in front of a steep staircase that led to a landing facing the windows; three doors there spoke to bedrooms and a possible bath.

Not having a search warrant meant I couldn't *legally* enter the premises, but I did "accidentally" try the sliding glass door. It was locked, but I was reasonably certain I didn't need to snoop any further inside the cottage. After taking a moment to appreciate the view from the porch once more – the longer I was there, the more comfortable I was becoming with how precariously close the cliff the cottage was located, it seemed – I walked back to the front of the house, then over to the small one-car garage just off to one side. It appeared to me as though it were a recent addition, or a conversion, perhaps, of a smaller unit the kids (or the servants, for that matter) might have used back in the day. Though fitted out in cedar shakes and green trim identical to the main cottage, there were no windows and only the fairly modern garage door attempting to appear as though it was a faux barn door.

The small beige remote for the door opener nearly blended in with the trim, but when I found it, I slipped on the pair of latex gloves I'd brought and then flipped the lid up to expose the keypad. Knowing most consumers fail to change the default passwords on their internet routers – or, in this case, garage door openers – I punched the standard *1 – 2 – 3 – 4* into the keypad and stood back as the portal slowly chugged open.

With the sun on the far side of the house and low enough that I was in the shade, I enabled the flashlight on my iPhone and smiled as I trained it on the space.

Television? Check.

Family silver? Check.

Work of art from (is that a Rembrandt? Damn!) -- Check.

Desktop computer? Check.

Getting down on my haunches, I pulled out my notebook and confirmed the serial number on the back of the tower. As I suspected, it matched with the one that had been stolen from the mansion. Except, of course, it hadn't been stolen at all.

I'd found everything pretty much where I expected to; as I snapped some photos on my phone, it left me with the larger, more obvious question: why had Rosie faked the robbery? Standing and then punching in the code to the door, I decided it wasn't to support the murder of Lillianna. While I had no evidence to back it up – yet – my hunch was Rosie had been surprised to find her housekeeper dead.

Except... wouldn't her housekeeper have noticed the missing items?

My confident steps back to the SUV faltered, for while I'd solved one part of the puzzle, a new one had merrily stepped up to take its place. Standing there in the quiet solitude of the property, I mulled it over and realized Lillianna herself had to have been in on the fake robbery. Smiling slightly, I felt pretty comfortable that were we to dust for prints, I'd find two sets on all of the items – for what loyal, lifelong servant wouldn't help her mistress when asked?

Damn, I thought. *This is going to be one interesting conversation with Rosie when I get back.*

As I pulled out of the cottage and headed back to the village, my thoughts hit on one final nugget. Why hadn't Mark driven up here? It was a conundrum that needed answering, and I wondered if I would find it as I delved into the cobweb-heavy second part of my assignment.

Sixteen

My normal internal alarm clock clicked off at four-thirty, and I rolled out of the extremely uncomfortable hotel bed, snapping the lamp on as I stretched the kinks out of my back. *Hotel* didn't quite describe where Travel had booked me, for the aging roadside structure I'd finally located on the outskirts of Saint Lucie looked to be a modestly renovated motel from the golden age of road trips; the neon sign had long been replaced by a more corporate looking logo, to be sure, but the bones of the place still spoke to a Route Sixty-Six vibe.

And that wasn't entirely good.

The room was tiny, presumably built for a period when the travelling public themselves were smaller and far more svelte. Unfortunately, the room felt even further cramped by the addition of furniture designed to make it appear it could be used by business travelers: a tiny desk, with non-functional internet jacks, had been crammed against the wall, opposite the foot of the double bed. A smaller table for two was wedged under the window to the outside, blocking the air conditioner and littered with pamphlets for local attractions, pizza parlors and take out from an Asian restaurant the next town over. Under the desk, a college dorm fridge that wheezed like an asthmatic had been stashed where presumably one would normally put their feet. As near as I could tell, there was no chair for the desk, nor any coffee for the coffee maker in the bathroom; I did, however, have two ironing boards (but no iron).

I wasn't looking forward to trying to get under the showerhead in the tub; designed for someone closer to four feet tall, the water was likely to hit me about the bellybutton. I was seriously considering just packing up and heading home, but my inner fitness geek won out. As the dresser was also missing, I hadn't bothered to unpack; my duffel was on the desk, and I dug through it to get my running gear. About the only positive thing the motel had going for it was location: from what the extremely cute check-in clerk had told me, the sidewalk was well lit all the way to town. He'd handed me a map that showed five- and ten-kilometer loops; when I got back to my room, I discovered he'd also scribbled down his number on the back.

For once, I'd opted to ignore the advance.

Locking the room behind me, I jogged out to the street and started uphill toward the main part of Saint Lucie. It was a bit chilly – okay, it was *a lot chilly* – and it took most of the first mile to warm up. By the second mile, I could see the buildings looming ahead of me in the lightening sky; as I hit the third, I found myself at the parking lot for the small independent grocer that was the only game in town. To my surprise, it was actually open at five in the morning; seeing that I'd neglected to bring a bottle of water with me (oh, wait, that was missing from the room, too), I walked through the sliding door into a brightly lit space.

Two small checkout lanes with belts were off to one side, and a traditional set of grocery departments wrapped around the perimeter of the space. Despite how small it was, somehow it managed to cram in a bakery, a meat department and a full deli. All of those areas were dark, though I could see an older woman putting something into the commercial oven behind the bakery counter. It took me a moment to find the coolers and snag a bottle of water; as I wandered back toward the register, the grandmotherly figure was placing pastries inside the display.

I caught a whiff of fresh bread and stopped short. "That smells unbelievably good," I said admiringly.

"I've got some loaves coming out in ten, if you want to wait. And bagels in less time."

"You had me at bread," I laughed, "but I have no self-control when it comes to bagels."

"Me either," she smiled. "Plain, cinnamon raisin or sesame?"

"Cinnamon, please."

"Stay right there and I'll grab it for you."

I hung out in front of the bakery for a bit, watching the only other person in range as she shuttled back and forth filling items in one aisle or another. The checkouts remained empty, but I presumed someone would magically appear when I trundled up there with my treasure. It was hard not to see the similarities between that grocery store and the one Sean's ex-fiancé had been running in Windeport. Both had the small, cozy feel of an establishment where the clerk knew who you were and what cut of meat you were likely to buy based on the day of the week or the month of the year. The oversized Von's I'd stopped into in Anaheim had no traces of that at all.

"Here you are, hon," the clerk said, reappearing with a small brown bag carefully folded over at the top.

"Thanks," I smiled. "This place reminds me of my old home," I added.

"I figured you weren't from around here," she said.

"What gave me away? The tights?"

"Being up at this hour," she chuckled. "Hon, I know everyone in this town and the earliest *anyone* gets up is six."

That made me smile. "Ah. Busted, it seems."

"Here for the weekend?"

"Sadly, no. I'm an investigator from Rancho Linda, south of Los Angeles."

Her eyes went wide. "Private?"

"No, I'm with the department. Trying to tie up some loose ends on a case I'm working. I'm headed back south this morning."

"What kind of case?"

"Property. Theft, mainly."

She nodded – I finally saw the name badge said *Barb* as she regarded me. "Found what you needed, then?"

"I think so," I smiled. "I suppose you get tons of tourists up here. But you still know everyone? Even seasonal visitors?"

"For sure," she smiled back, for clearly it was a point of pride. "We're the closest grocery store – well, actually the *only* one for about twenty miles. Everyone has to shop here."

A thought struck me. "Don't take this the wrong way, but how long have you worked here?"

That made her cackle. "Probably since before you were born," she laughed. "Early eighties."

"Do you know Dr. Frankenhoffer?"

Barb's eyes lit up. "Rosie? Oh God yes. She's a breath of fresh air whenever she spends time up here." She looked wistful for a bit. "I hadn't been here long when she bought that cabin up the coast; for decades, she used to spend May to September up there, polishing her latest work."

"I understand it's quite a place."

"It is. She's renovated it a bit, of course, 'cause the place dates back to the early thirties."

"You've been there?"

"Oh yeah," she smiled. "You know, she was the most ordinary person? When she was here in the summer, she'd host parties up there for the entire town each Thursday, and a huge Fourth of July thing that was a joy to behold. Those parties were the only time you knew she had money, but damn, she never lorded it over anyone. She was so... normal? If that makes sense." That wistful look reappeared. "Rosie hasn't been up much since her heart issues, though. Surprised the hell out of me a few weeks back when she suddenly turned up, I can tell you that."

I nodded, checking another box in my mental notebook. "Up for the weekend, was she?"

"I think so," she said, brow furrowing. "Maybe? I usually work three days a week now – I'm trying to retire but haven't pulled the trigger yet – and I'm sure I saw her on a Thursday." Barb looked at me. "You know Rosie?"

"We... swim together down in Rancho Linda."

Barb's eyes went to my exposed biceps. "I'll bet. Did you know she just missed the team back in the sixties?"

"I didn't," I said. "I've only just met her."

"She hardly ever talks about it. But ask her and she will." She looked at me again. "You know, I have the strangest feeling we've met before."

I smiled. "It's the hair," I laughed, knowing otherwise considering how NBC Sports had done an exhaustive bio on me of that aired both on television and had been on the web. "I'm often mistaken for some Hollywood actor I don't even know."

"Huh," she said. "That's probably it."

"It usually is," I laughed.

Seventeen

I left Saint Lucie mid-morning and made reasonably good time traveling south. The traffic in Los Angeles wasn't rush hour-quality when I hit it about two, but it was still heavy enough that I managed to waste a full hour despite attempting to be more tactical in navigating around the worst of it. The final leg down to Anaheim and then over to Rancho Linda was the smoothest part of the trip, though by the time I finally arrived, it was late enough in the day shift it seemed a bit like I was just putting in a pro forma appearance at the station.

Actually, that wasn't fair, for technically I'd been on the clock from the moment I left to the moment I arrived back at the station. Still, that didn't stop me from getting a fresh cup of coffee and settling in to update the case file with what I had uncovered. I was putting the finishing touches on my commentary and about to work on my receipts for Travel when my phone buzzed.

"Detective Korsokovach."

"Detective, you're back."

"Yes, Chief," I said, pausing in my typing. "It was productive, I think. Do you want a rundown?"

"I assume since you're still here long after hours, I can read the summary in the file later tonight," he laughed. Only then did I see it was well past seven. "I should warn you, I didn't authorize any overtime for this case."

"Sorry, Chief," I replied. "I guess I lost track of time updating the system."

"Go home, Vasily. I'll catch you first thing."

"Of course, Chief."

As I hung up, I wondered what Mark would say about Chief Andrews himself burning the midnight oil. Given how he seemed to have an axe to grind (for what reason I was still uncertain), the very fact the Chief was still putting in fourteen-hour days this close to retirement said something to *me* about the man's dedication. Still, he'd kind of given me a direct order, so I wrapped up the form I was on, slid my laptop back into my backpack and headed out.

Hungry but not feeling like cooking, I swung by a natural foods grocer and picked up one of those rotisserie chickens that seemed to be perennially available. Snagging a fresh salad and half a watermelon, I continued on to my condo. Nearly two days on the road had taken a bit out of me, so a nice, quiet evening to catch up on my Netflix queue seemed to be in order. The most recent season of *Miraculous* – at least, the first part of the most recent season – had dropped, and I'd been delaying streaming it since I knew it would cut out at the half-way mark.

That got me thinking that I still had half a season of *Outlander* left to go, too. The hunk playing Jamie was, of course, the main attraction for me, but the subplot with Lord John also seemed a bit too close to home and therefore worth following. I could completely relate to a character who was in love with someone incapable of returning that affection, and though I knew it was only fiction, I was curious to see how the relationship evolved over the course of the series. Maybe there were some pointers there I could use – assuming I ever found myself back in that situation again.

Unlocking the door to my condo, I paused in the hallway to pick up a note on the tile. Unfolding it, I could see it was from the building superintendent; I had asked him to oversee the appliance and furniture deliveries while I was upstate, and the note confirmed it had taken place. The bright white of the washer/dryer combo made me smile – clean clothes were in my future, now – but the prospect of a solid night's rest on a quality mattress seemed incredibly attractive.

Setting down my food, I hurried to the master bedroom and snapped on the light. The king-sized bed loomed large in the space, far larger than I'd realized it would be. I'd never had a bed that big before and to be honest would have been happy with a queen had the salesperson not told me it was only an extra hundred for the upgrade. Who was I to argue with value?

Except, as I stood there, I realized I'd forgotten to get sheets while I was out. Feeling too tired to go back out again, I threw the comforter I did have on it and called it good.

I stripped off my informal uniform and slid into my sleeping pants, then padded out to the kitchen to enjoy dinner. As I sliced up the chicken to put into my salad, I thought about how I wanted to tackle the next part of the investigation. Meeting with Rosie was high on that list, but I needed to do some background on the former occupant, too.

Munching on a tomato plucked from the salad, I considered for a moment how much information I wanted to get out of Chief Andrews, versus how much I wanted to know in advance. One thing I had learned over years of working with Sean had been that the more data you had in your pocket, the more informed your questions could be. The Chief wasn't a suspect – at least, I had no earthly reason to suspect he had something to do with the possible murder of his grandfather – but the principle held. I did get a slight chuckle seeing him as a toddler pushing his forebear into the pool.

That made me curious, though, and I slid my laptop out of the backpack I'd casually dropped at the edge of the breakfast bar. A quick search landed me on the homepage for the Rancho Linda Public Library; like most across the nation, many of its resources were available online to patrons. But as I quickly found out, I *wasn't* in that category quite yet and therefore was banned from looking through the back issues of the local newspaper. A quick check of their hours told me I'd missed them by a mile, so I made a mental note to rectify the situation in the morning. If I was lucky, I might run into that same reference librarian I'd met earlier.

I swapped over to the streaming services and queued up Miraculous, deciding a little anime was the right way to wind down the day; it was not meant to be, for my iPhone buzzed just a few minutes into the episode where the heroes swapped their magical jewels by accident. It was a controversial one that I'd been looking forward to, and I frowned deeper when I saw who the interrupting party was.

"Mark," I said after answering.

"What are you doing tonight?" he asked. There was a heavy baseline throbbing in the background, accompanied by what seemed like some sort of muted electronica. Unless I missed my mark, he was at one of the many gay nightclubs in the area.

"Watching a movie," I lied, not particularly sure why.

"Jesus, dude. Get that hot ass of yours down here."

"Where is 'here' exactly?"

"Santa Monica. Just off the pier. Club Penguin."

"I'm not a dancer," I replied. "And it's late."

"Come *on*," he implored. "I need you here."

"You won't die without me."

"Just *thinking* about wrapping my hand around that bubble ass of yours is getting me hard," he said. "Are you sure you don't want my undivided attention?"

Oddly, I *was* having a physical response to the conversation as attested to by the sudden tenting of my sleeping pants. Having once had his hands all over me made it quite easy to fantasize how it would happen again.

Shit.

"Not tonight," I replied.

"You are *such* a tease," he accused. "Damn. Painfully so."

I frowned, slightly concerned about his tone; it was borderline accusatory. "Look, I'm tired and I'm going to bed as soon as this movie is over. Enjoy your evening."

"Dammit--!" he howled as I cut him off.

Putting the phone down on the counter, it was close to ten at that point; as I had practice to get to in the morning, I tossed the remains of my dinner into the trash and trundled off to my bedroom. After going through my nightly ablutions, I slipped into the comforter and luxuriated in not being on the ground for the first time in nearly a week (not counting whatever that had been in the motel).

It occurred to me a pillow, and maybe sheets, would have made it better. But at that point, I was tired enough not to care and just slipped off to sleep.

Eighteen

With Drew being out of town, breakfast at the diner felt awkward.

The same host was there, of course, seating me in the same booth I'd been frequenting nearly every day since moving to California. I finally learned her name was Antonia, actually, but our conversation was as brief as always. Staring at the menu seemed stupid since I knew what I was going to order, but when a young blonde woman appeared, she frowned when I asked for my usual oatmeal and berries.

"We don't serve that," she said.

"Actually, you do," I smiled.

"We don't," she insisted.

"I--" I started, and saw she was getting agitated. Wondering if she was just new, and not wanting to push the issue, I ordered an omelet and called it good; it seemed to relieve her greatly, but I worried for her future in the hospitality business.

After she left my cup of coffee (and having taken the carafe with her), I smiled wanly at how I missed my new friend. Hoping he was having a good time with his *actual* boyfriend, I turned to the window to watch the early portion of the rush hour bustle on the road in front of the diner. I caught my reflection in the glass, backlit in the semi-darkness of the early hour; I'd not shaved before driving down from Saint Lucie, and had come straight from the pool with the plan to shower at the station. As I ran a hand over the stubble, I smiled slightly, for it was something I'd long wanted to do – the cool, unshaved look – but it had felt out of place in Maine. California, on the other hand, was the land of casual. Turning my face from side to side, I decided I'd give it a shot and see how long it lasted before the inevitable itching got to me.

Suddenly I was reminded of the agony the week after shaving down for a meet, and shuddered just as my omelet arrived. My server just looked at me and left without even refilling my coffee mug. Deciding I'd overstayed my welcome, I snarfed down the rather awful egg concoction and hurriedly paid the tab before driving to the station.

Freshly showered and behind my desk a bit before seven, I was just logging into my computer when Mark rounded the edge of the cubicle row. "Hey gorgeous," he said as he leaned down and nibbled at my ear.

"Hey!" I said as I pulled away from him. "*Not* appropriate!"

"I missed you, too," he said as he took off his sportscoat and leaned on his desk. "How was upstate?"

I swiveled my chair to face him. "Good. Any reason why you didn't go up yourself?"

"No reason to do it," he shrugged. "Frankenhoffer gave me receipts for gas, so it wasn't like she couldn't prove she'd made the trip."

"Did she?" I asked. "I don't recall seeing those in the file."

"I'm sure they were there," he said, but the look on his face told me I'd caught him. "They should be," he insisted, more to himself as he turned to his desk. Pulling open a drawer, he rustled around a bit until he came up with a batch of paper clipped with one of those oversized things normally reserved for bags of potato chips. "Here," he said, handing it to me. "I guess I forgot to scan them."

Flipping through the paperwork, I could see originals for fuel and food receipts covering the dates Rosie was in Saint Lucie. "Any other treasures in there?" I asked as I put the batch on my desk.

"No," he said.

"Are you sure?" I pressed. "So far, I'm not terribly impressed with your filing skills."

Something flashed across his face, and he stepped over to me, leaning down. "I can file just fine, thank you," he smiled. "Are you free tonight?"

"Why?"

"Dinner. Then sex."

I shook my head. "Well, at least food is involved this time."

"Is that a yes?"

"It depends on how the day goes."

"Six?" he pressed.

"We'll see," I said.

"Your place?"

"What do you do when someone says 'no?'"

"They don't, generally," he laughed. "Text me, then?"

"Maybe I will," I replied as he pulled his coat back on.

"Tease," he accused as he rounded the corner and was gone.

I shook my head again, wondering for the millionth time what it was, exactly, he did. For being a detective didn't seem very high on his list. Turning back to my desk, I sipped on my coffee and poked at the virtual in-out board; the Chief's indicator was still "out" making me wonder if his definition of *first thing* was closer to lunchtime. Pulling up the library website, I saw I still had a few hours before they opened and found myself at a weird crossroads.

Rosie hadn't been at practice that morning, which had put a wrench into my day. I'd hoped to snag her after we'd finished at the pool so I could tease out of her the true story of what happened to her computer, reluctant as I was to go another round in the solarium. But the overlapping case did require me to visit her mansion once more, so I sighed, resigned to having to quite literally sweat it out of her. Or me.

That made me smile slightly, for I thought I might just have the right outfit for just such an occasion. I caught up on my email and did my Information Security Awareness training to round out the hour, not wanting to call before eight. A few minutes after, I dialed her number.

It rang several times and went to a mechanical answering machine; my eyebrows went up when I realized it was an old-fashioned tape version, for I could hear the hissing in the background. I started to leave a message, looked at the clock again and did some math.

What the hell.

Hanging up, I grabbed my laptop and duffel; ducking into the locker room for the second time that day, I quickly changed into clean muscle tank and matching running tights, adding a coordinated microfiber short since I needed the pockets. Then it was back to the SUV and on the road, fighting the full-on rush hour traffic of Rancho Linda to work my way back to the mansion on the hill.

The hulking home seemed more foreboding the second time around as I pulled the SUV up to the curb in front of the massive double front door. I assumed it was because I now suspected some level of evil had taken place inside those walls, but as I slid out of the front seat and pushed my hair back with my sunglasses, something else felt off. Striding up the steps to the front door, I leaned on the doorbell and waited expectantly for her housekeeper to appear.

As seconds stretched into minutes, that nagging feeling became more prominent. My hand went to my hip only to remember I'd left my service weapon locked up in the SUV – it hadn't meshed with my athletic attire, and now I was wishing I'd not been planning to use my physical assets to elicit the truth from a possible suspect. Torn for a moment, I forged ahead anyway, ringing the doorbell again. I waited another full minute before jogging back to the SUV and retrieving my weapon. Slowly, I started to jog around the perimeter of the mansion, Glock down, and tried to quell the feeling that something awful had happened.

A small driveway peeled off one edge of the loop, and I ran down it to find a four-car garage and what appeared to be small side lot, presumably for the hired help. No cars were there and peering through the windows to the garage netted me only the flivver I'd seen Rosie in at the pool. That meant she was still at home.

Continuing my circuit, I came to the solarium, but the windows were as fogged up as ever; determining if she were inside was fruitless and I didn't yet have enough probable cause to smash a window. But as my concern grew, I started to think health and safety was quickly becoming a frontrunner. I kept jogging, past a small, squat outbuilding just a few feet from the solarium. It seemed a bit newer than the mansion itself, but also fit in with the aesthetics of the grounds, surrounding by manicured bushes and lush plantings.

One more corner and I was on the petite patio outside of Rosie's small writing room; the curtains had been pulled back from the tall glass windows, and as I pressed my hands to look through, here too there didn't seem to be much to see. I started to pull back until I caught what looked like a flip-flop by the edge of her desk. One I'd seen at the pool before.

Squinting, I thought it was possible the flip-flop was still connected to foot.

Not wanting to damage my weapon, I slid the Glock into the rear of my waistband then hastily looked around, quickly locating a relatively flat, medium-sized river rock from the small Zen-like garden; hefting it, I held it in one hand, then turned slightly away from the tall pane of glass before smashing it with the rock and ducking out of the way of the falling shards. It took but a moment, but it felt longer; I hurtled over what was left and made my way behind the desk.

Rosie was on her side, wearing the warmup gear she'd sported once or twice at practice. One arm was flung forward, and her cell phone was a few feet further in that direction, speaking to one possibility of what had happened. I quickly looked for injuries but found nothing visible. Her eyes were closed, but her skin didn't have the pallor of a cadaver – at least, not yet. Dropping to my knees, I pressed a hand to her neck and felt for a pulse. Her skin was cold but not rubbery, which gave me some minimal hope. Holding my breath, I waited a moment before repositioning my fingers; it felt like an eternity before I finally found it, weak and thready.

I slid my iPhone out from the pocket of my shorts and immediately dialed 9-1-1.

Nineteen

"That'll teach me."

I sat at the edge of the hospital bed in the ICU of the Orange County Medical Center and gently smiled at Rosie, who was looking far better than when I'd found her nearly eight hours earlier. Angled upward in the bed and wearing an awful looking jumper from the hospital, she had wires, tubes and cables running from her to any number of machines. Despite having seen her at the pool, she seemed frail sitting there with an oxygen line hooked over her ears and pressed to her nose.

"And what would that be?" I asked. I was feeling a bit lightheaded myself, having skipped lunch to ensure I'd be there when she'd awoken from emergency surgery.

"My cardiologist said the battery in that thing was due for an upgrade. I thought I could put it off another year – who wants to voluntarily go under the knife? But clearly it was deader than a doornail." She sighed. "Lousy time for my new housekeeper to be taking some vacation."

I nodded, having heard a version of this from the surgeon earlier. It had been difficult to pry anything out of him, given I wasn't family;

flashing my badge hadn't gotten me anywhere, either, though I couldn't really blame the doctor. Standing there in my running gear had undercut my professionalism immensely; it was only after Chief Andrews appeared and spoke with the director of the Emergency Room that they became more forthcoming. It helped they were both members of the Rotary, it seemed.

Also in my favor was Rosie's lack of next of kin. They'd needed someone to make a decision while she'd been unconscious, and I'd stepped in. It was partially self-serving, for I needed my suspect/witness alive; but I also had grown a bit fond of her as a person, and for some reason really wanted her to pull through. Which she had.

"Maybe you'll listen to him next time?" I asked, arms folded against my muscle shirt. Like most hospitals, the air conditioning seemed to be set to sub-zero, but I'd been loath to leave and change before getting her back to the world.

"For sure," she sighed. "Two hours?"

I nodded. "It took them at least that long to stabilize you after I found you. They think you went down this morning?"

"About four-thirty," she nodded. "I was writing – I'd had a thought about a section and wanted to get it done before practice – but right in the middle of it I had this twinge that didn't feel right. It worried me a bit since they'd told me the defibrillator was nearly undetectable when it fired off. I was in the groove, though, and did what they always tell you *not* to do and kept going until there was another twinge; that one was a doozy, enough to reach for the phone and call for help." She looked out the window at the fading light of the early evening. "That's the last thing I remember, before I woke up here," she continued, turning back to me. "Looking into those handsome eyes of yours."

I smiled. "Your a-fib knocked you for a loop and you passed out. It was sheer luck there was enough juice left in your defib gizmo that it kept you going until I got there."

"No kidding," she said soberly. "I can't believe I've slept most of the day."

"Well, you needed your rest. They had to do a full replacement, removing your old unit and upgrading you to the latest model. Not a trivial endeavor."

"Of course they did," she chuckled, before grimacing. "My insurance company is gonna love this. And man, it hurts to laugh."

I decided not to tell her that they'd nearly lost her on the ride in from the mansion; I was sure the CPR they'd done to her had bruised a rib or two. "I, for one, am glad to see you awake."

"It's nice of you to hang around, but surely you have more important things to do than see an old codger through her surgery. You must have a date or something tonight."

I smiled, thinking of Mark and our quasi-planned evening ahead. "Sort of," I said.

"Is she cute?"

"Who?" I asked, puzzled.

"Your girlfriend."

"Oh," I said, flushing slightly. "You didn't look me up, did you?"

It was her turn to be confused. "Why would I do that?"

"Most people Google me and know my entire background," I explained.

"I don't know what that is – isn't that a large number or something? And why would that have anything to do with your girlfriend?"

I sidled up closer to her. "I forgot that you don't exist in the same world the rest of us do," I laughed. "I think that's why I like you so much."

"I still don't---"

"I'm gay, Rosie. And it was rather spectacularly on display when I was competing at the Olympics. I just assumed you knew."

Despite looking like she had just undergone surgery, Rosie's face went several shades of red. "Oh, Vasily, I'm so sorry. People of my generation, we just make assumptions – dear God, I'm terribly embarrassed."

"Don't be," I laughed as I leaned down and hugged her. "I'm not. Haven't been for a long time now."

Rosie laughed. "Well, okay then. Let me correct myself: is *he* cute?"

"Very," I said as I pulled away, "but we're not quite to the boyfriend stage. Technically it's just---"

"I think we'll leave it right there," she laughed before gripping her side.

"I should go," I said, looking at my watch. "But I need to ask you a couple of questions if you are up to it."

"Go for it," she replied.

"Did Lillianna help you stage the robbery?"

Rosie blinked, and the flush deepened. "Shit," she said, smiling ruefully. "You figured it out, didn't you?"

I nodded. "And found the computer and other goodies up at your cottage. Nice view, by the way."

"It is," she said, leaning back and closing her eyes. "How much trouble am I in?"

"None, if this is just a big misunderstanding," I said. "I can't speak for your publisher, of course..."

Rosie opened her eyes and caught mine. "I'm not ready to be done," she said, "but my contract ends with this last book. My agent has told me that despite my track record, no house wants me due to my age."

"The book's done, isn't it?"

She nodded. "Six years ago, to be honest. I'm writing the next one right now, actually. I've been doing research into the intersection of herbal medicines and its effects on the polytheistic religions of Machu Picchu."

"You want my advice?"

"Sure," she said.

"Self-publish. It's pretty damn easy these days and I would be willing to bet someone with your cachet – and loyal readers – would have a pretty easy time of it."

"I don't know the first thing about it," she said.

"I know some people," I replied, thinking of Charlie back in Windeport. "I'll ask around if you like. But then you get that last book out and immediately follow it up with your next one."

Rosie looked at me. "You really think someone like me – an old broad in the twilight of her career – can pull that off?"

"I heard you were nearly an Olympian yourself," I replied. "I happen to know what it takes to get to that level. I'm sure you can do this – if you want to."

"Well," she smiled slightly, "it certainly is something to think about."

"Good. Now, tell me what really happened the night you got back from Saint Lucie."

Her eyes snapped to mine. "You don't think I killed poor Lillianna, do you?"

"I don't know *what* to think, Rosie," I said as I slid my iPhone from my pocket and started to record our conversation. "This is just for the file," I said.

"All right." Pausing for a beat, she continued. "It pretty much happened as I described it initially, save for the staged robbery. Yes, Lillianna helped me pack the car with everything that was to be stolen, and I did take it all to my cottage upstate."

"I've already confirmed you were there," I said. "You drove back...?"

"I parked my car in the garage at the mansion but was surprised when she didn't meet me. Normally she's waiting so she can take up my bags – I hated that she insisted on doing it, as old as she was, but she wouldn't hear of it."

"She'd been with you a long time."

"Oddly, she'd begun to talk about retiring only recently. I'd set aside a nice chunk for her to do so, actually; after all those years putting up with me, it was precious little recompense I think." Rosie shifted in her bed. "The garage connects to the kitchen, and the first sign something was wrong was her half-prepared dinner sitting on the counter. She never ate in that room – always in her personal quarters, so that was enough for me to start calling out her name."

Rosie looked out the window. "I don't know why, but the writing room was the first place I looked. Call it a powerful sense of dread or something; whatever it was, I hurried down the hallway and found her."

"In the writing room?" I asked pointedly.

"Yes," she said. "Quite dead, I assure you."

"And you saw the... blow... to the back of her head?"

"Yes," she said again, looking at me askance. "I'm not crazy. I found her where I showed the responding officer."

"I'm sure you did," I said. "It's just that, well, that kind of wound tends to leave a lot of blood behind. And there was next to none in that room."

Rosie looked at me. "She didn't die there, did she?"

"I don't think so," I replied. "Besides Lillianna, who else knew you were going to Saint Lucie?"

"No one," she said. "Well, that's not true. The agency that supplies the chef and gardener knew, just in case something came up."

"Anyone else?"

"No," she replied.

"Okay then," I said as I clicked off the recorder and leaned down to kiss her on the forehead. "I'll check on you in the morning. And – no arguments, please – I'll be the one to take you back to the mansion when you check out of this cozy bed-and-breakfast." I paused. "I need to snoop around your home again. Do I have your permission to--"

"Hell yes," she said. "I want to know what happened as badly as you seem to."

"Good," I smiled as I slid off the bed. "Get some rest and I'll see you tomorrow."

"I will." Her voice caught me at the door. "Vasily?"

I turned.

"I'll be honest, I was a little surprised that her death didn't get much of an investigation."

"Me, too," I replied. "But that's about to change."

Twenty

Unsurprisingly, Mark was waiting in the garage when I pulled into my spot at the complex, leaning against an extremely stereotypical recent model year Mustang. Much as the last time he'd been there, he was attired in a compression shirt, leggings and shorts, though he didn't appear to be drunk this time.

Locking the SUV, I saw him smile as I walked over to him with my duffel and backpack. "I'm starting to feel like I am just your post-workout recovery program," I said, seeing his shirt was still damp in spots and his hair was matted.

Pulling me to him, he roughly pressed his lips to mine, cupping my ass with his hand; the shock of his actions led me to drop my duffel. As he leaned back, I could see he was wearing a smile and a feral look that gave me pause.

"Why mess with a winning formula," he asked as he ran his hand from my ass up beneath my muscle tee to press me closer to him.

Given our location, I began to protest only to have it smothered in another urgent kiss. I was starting to discover that the mingling of sweat, deodorant and the musky smell of desire was something of an aphrodisiac for me, despite the very real misgivings I was having about his aggressively domineering approach.

Deciding to flip the situation, I leaned into him, pressing his back up and over the rear of his car as I snaked a hand up the leg of his shorts. Finding I had his full attention in more ways than one, I gently squeezed and was rewarded with a moan and tiny shudder. "Whoa, tiger," he said huskily as he tried to push me away.

Slowly, I started to work him over with one hand, bracing my other arm against his chest to keep him pinned. The angle and the weight of my body worked against him, and as he started to try and squirm away from me, I knew he was close. "Now, do I finish this here?" I asked softly, leaning up into his ear, "or are you gonna be a good boy and let me have some dinner first, like you promised?"

"Jesus! Not here!" he whined.

"Really?" I moved my lower hand one more time very, *very* slowly. "Are you sure?"

"*Yes*!" he cried out with anguish.

Pulling myself off him, I picked up the gear I had dropped when he'd made his move and started toward the elevators. I heard Mark swear multiple times behind me before jogging to catch up. "Give me a bag," he demanded as we approached the doors to the elevator lobby.

"Why--" I started to ask before seeing the reason on the front of his shorts. "Ah," I smiled, maybe a touch cruelly. Handing him my duffel, I half-heartedly apologized. "Sorry. But you can't go around attacking people like that without expecting consequences."

"My revenge will be sweet," he said darkly as I waved my fob at the sensor and turned to see the oddest look upon his face.

"Let's get one thing straight," I said as we stepped into the elevator, with him trying to remain serious as he held the bag awkwardly in front of him. "*You* are pursuing *me*. You may recall I told you I wasn't interested in a relationship at the moment; if you want this to work, you need to know it will *only* work if you consider me an equal." I stepped closer to him. "I have *never* been someone's sub, and that won't change just because you've managed to fuck me already."

Mark's eyes widened. "You've got some spirit," he said, still breathing a bit heavy from the garage.

"I don't know what you're used to, Mark, but I ain't it," I quipped in my best Maine accent. As the lift slowed and the doors opened on my floor, I paused in the entrance. "Do you understand?"

He nodded and followed me down the hallway to my condo. As I unlocked the door, I turned to him. "Where's dinner?" I asked, pausing at the threshold.

Looking sheepish, Mark hung his head. "I... thought we'd go out after..." he trailed off.

"Seriously?" I sighed, my eyes drifting down to his shorts and the spreading stain. "Well, you can't go out like that now, can you? And I suppose you don't have any *other* clothes with you?"

He shook his head.

"You are a terrible planner. Come on in," I sighed again. "I hope you like pasta."

Putting my gear down in the living room, Mark added my bag to the stack and slid onto a barstool facing me as I started to pull out a jar of sauce and a pack of fresh sausage ravioli I'd picked up earlier. "I'm... sorry," Mark choked out, his green eyes catching mine. "I'm used to taking what I want."

"I can tell," I snorted. "And how many relationships have you burned through as a result?"

"Plenty," he said. "You're something altogether different, as intoxicating as the most addictive drug. I *need* you in a way I've never felt before."

"Puh-lease," I said, rolling my eyes as I put the sauce on and filled a pot full of water. "I'm just a new, exotic flavor."

"Maybe," he laughed. "But one that I desperately have to have more of," he added, leaning up and over the counter, clearly angling for a kiss.

I tapped him on the lips with a finger. "Down, boy," I smiled.

"Shit," he said, that dark expression washing over him again. "You *are* a tease, and it's going to get you into trouble someday."

I looked over the ravioli as I opened the package. "I can handle you, lover boy," I smiled.

"Can you?" he asked, a sly smile appearing. "I'd like to test that."

"In your dreams," I laughed, but those warning bells were going off again. I shoved them to the back of my brain again and got busy making dinner.

Not apparently wanting to concede the point, Mark slid off the barstool and came into the kitchen proper; coming up behind me, he wrapped his arms around my chest and pressed himself into my back. The shock of the dampness against my ass was overridden by my surprise at his obvious desire. "You recharge fast," I observed.

"How long until dinner is ready?" he asked in my ear, nibbling at the lobe.

Sighing, I turned down the sauce, lowered the temp and put the ravioli on the sideboard, realizing he wasn't going to let me be until I knocked the edge off the evening. "Long enough," I said as I turned toward him.

Much tugging of spandex followed, leaving a trail of workout material from the kitchen to my new bed; I'd barely had time to spread the comforter and retrieve two condoms from the nightstand before we were on to the main event. Unlike our first time together, Mark was far more forceful; whether it was payback for what had transpired in the garage or not, I wasn't sure, but my repeated attempts to keep our ministrations on an equal footing became increasingly difficult.

Those warning bells went to a full-on red alert when he maneuvered a leg under me and, using what I assumed was some sort of wrestling move, managed to quickly flip me onto my face. "Hey!" I said, a bit shocked as he drove my face into the mattress, pinning my arms beneath me. "What the hell--" I started before he reached his big hand around and silenced me.

"Shut the fuck up," he veritably growled as he pressed his body against mine, leveraging his bulk to keep me from moving. Using his free hand, he started to guide himself into me, and not in a gentle way.

Realizing I was about to be forcibly raped, multiple thoughts ran through my mind, one of them being the tiny voice that had been telling me all along this guy was bad news. The other was, of all things, anger that my sauce was likely to burn if I didn't get out of this situation quickly. I tried to squirm out of his embrace again, netting very little; instead, Mark clamped his hand tighter, covering both mouth *and* nose, then actually pulled my head back to an extremely uncomfortable angle.

"As I said, I take what I want," he laughed cruelly as I tried unsuccessfully to breathe. "And I *want* a piece of your ass."

Blackness crept in on the edge of my vision, though as a swimmer, I was quite capable of going for a minute or more without air. Still, as I tried to twist away from him, I realized it was quite different going twenty meters underwater versus fighting off an attacker intent on having his way with me. Trying to remain calm as he struggled a bit to enter me, I sorted through my options.

Swimming!

With what strength I still had, I did a full-body dolphin kick; butterfly was my best stroke, after all, and the motion was so unexpected from me that it shifted a surprised Mark to the side slightly. The angle was just right that it lifted some of the bulk of his weight from my back, enough that a second kick, combined with a massive push up from the mattress threw him completely off of me.

Training kicked in and I rolled away from his clawing hands as he tried to regain the upper hand. Landing on the floor, I harbored no illusions that this could get ugly very quickly and looked for any sort of weapon, though none were close at hand. Mark was still on the bed, but that didn't last; I managed to roll away from him a second time as he landed on the carpet with a dull thud.

Scrambling to get to my feet, I pulled myself around the door to the master and booked to the bar, grabbing my phone from where I'd left it on the counter. Turning on the video function, I put my back to the wall and held my iPhone as though it were on speaker, but keeping Mark in the frame as he came around and started to make a rush for me.

"This is Detective Vasily Korsokovach," I said loudly. "Requesting assistance--"

Mark skidded to a stop a few feet from me. "Don't do that," he said, holding up his hands. "It'll ruin both of us."

"Only *one* of us tried to rape the other," I said. "I should know, since I was on the receiving end."

"I misunderstood the signs," Mark replied, but it sounded lame even to his own ears. "I'll just leave, and we can forget this ever happened."

"I'm not sure that's possible, *Detective*," I said pointedly. "It goes without saying you're no longer welcome here."

I watched as his vaguely contrite expression shifted to a slight sneer. "You're not worth a second helping," he replied coldly, once more trying to shift our positions.

"That goes both ways, dude," I said. "Now get your gear and get the *hell* out of here."

I continued to hold the phone and watched as he slowly tugged on his leggings, then shorts and finally, deliberately, his shirt. His look told me he actually felt we had unfinished business, and I filed that away as he finally, quietly, backed out of the condo. Despite being naked, I kept myself glued to the wall, and waited until my pulse finally dropped back into a somewhat normal rhythm. I saved the video from my phone to the cloud and then sank to the carpet of my living room.

Deep in my heart, I knew this was going to be a problem. I just had no idea how *big* a problem it would become. Sighing, I knew there was something I needed to do to protect myself. Flipping through my contacts, I found Chief Andrews' number and dialed. He picked up on the second ring,

"Chief? Do you have a few minutes...?"

Twenty-One

I went to the hospital directly after swim practice, and found Rosie was sitting up and eating what passed for breakfast in the hospital. She caught me as I paused at the door, waiting to be invited in. "Hey," she smiled. "Come see what they want me to eat, and then tell me you've smuggled me an Egg McMuffin in your sweatshirt."

Smiling, I shook my head sadly. "I didn't get your emergency flare, sorry." I glanced down at what looked like a broth of some sort and a slice of something that stretched the very definition of toast to the limit. "What, exactly, is that?"

Rosie pushed the tray away. "Nothing I want."

"You've got to eat," I said reasonably.

"Bring me an Egg McMuffin, then," she rejoindered.

"I'll take that under advisement. How are you feeling?"

"Well, I'm tired of being poked and prodded and asked how I'm feeling," she replied a bit tartly. "But I know it comes with the territory." Rosie looked at me for a moment, then smiled slightly. "Did you get any rest yourself last night? That boyfriend of yours looks to have kept you busy."

"Something like that," I said airily as I pulled my still-damp hair back into a ponytail and did a quick casual knot to keep it out of the way.

I knew there was a hint of darkness around my eyes from lack of sleep; it *had* been a long night of self-recrimination, no small amount resulting in the ear-blistering dressing down I'd received from Chief Andrews. After his temperature cooled, he'd tactfully asked that I do field work for the day while he figured out what to do about my situation, which was more than fine with me. *That* led me to worries about what my future in Rancho Linda might look like, which fed the feedback loop of beating myself up for not disclosing Mark's advances sooner.

"I'm glad one of us is having fun, then," she laughed.

"What's the plan for today?" I asked, changing the subject as I leaned against the edge of her bed.

"You just missed the doctor, actually. A few tests, one of which involves some sort of download from my heart. If everything checks out, I might get to go home tonight."

"Good," I said, then added with a chuckle, "though I think they are downloading from your defibrillator. Not your heart. Unless you've become a cyborg in my absence."

"Same difference," she replied, arching an eyebrow.

That made me laugh. "I am out and about all day. I don't know if I can make it for lunch, but I'll definitely be here to take you home tonight if that is the solid plan."

"Sounds good," she smiled as I leaned down to kiss her forehead again.

"All right, I am off to pilfer through your home."

"If you find my spare set of reading glasses, let me know."

I gave her a thumbs-up as I left, thankful that she seemed more like herself.

Since I'd been temporarily banned from the station, I'd not bothered to dress the part of Police Officer, favoring a more casual look of nylon wind pants and an old sweatshirt with a faded UEM Men's Swimming logo on it. My badge was clipped to the waistband, and chafed rather uncomfortably. I felt like one of those television cops that went undercover in a high school, only to reveal themselves to their fellow students when the crime was going down; glancing in the rearview mirror, I was sad to note that my days of passing as a teenager were quite likely behind me.

The website for the library had contained a pleasant surprise when I'd given up sleeping and had started to work the case files again. Thursdays were the solo day of the week it opened at eight, allowing me to dig through some historical files before returning to the mansion for what I was fervently hoping would be the discovery of a solid clue (or two). I'd done some prep work, though, and had a list of dates for the local paper I wanted to read based on what information I'd been able to dig up via Google.

I also finally had a chance to review the contract Rosie had with her publisher, the electronic document having arrived in my inbox from the publisher's law firm well after Mark had scuttled out of the condo. It had been dense going, making me feel as though I'd been slogging through one of those massive End User License Agreements you were often forced to accept before using whatever software you were trying to download. Some areas, though, had been enlightening; while I'd need a forensic accountant to analyze the numbers side, my non-finance read of several portions told me Rosie was correct. While there was language of "right of first refusal" for any works after the final one, it was clear they wouldn't pay nearly the same amount as they'd done earlier in her career.

Reading between the lines, it was easy to tell that they felt her time had come. And gone.

Pulling into the parking lot of the library, I grabbed my backpack and locked the SUV; on my short walk to the door, I found the day had warmed rather quickly. I pulled off my sweatshirt and tucked it under an arm, then pulled open the massive oak door to enter the domain of scholars.

I was in luck, for the helpful reference librarian I had spoken to a few days earlier was on duty when I arrived at the massive semicircular Research Desk. I'd not caught her name the first time I'd been there, but as her head lifted at my approach, the smile on her face and her greeting told me she'd remembered me a little better.

"Detective Korsokovach," she said warmly as she stood from her rolling chair. "How are you this fine Thursday morning?" Her eyes quickly took in my attire, and a smile quirked at her thin lips. "Day off? Or is it casual day over at the station?"

For some reason, I'd not noticed her lipstick was a delicate shade of rose that matched her complexion perfectly. I understood feminine beauty in an intellectual way – enough that I could appreciate some of the finer examples from the opposite sex; Beverly (thank *God* she had a name badge on) was one of those, having the sort of natural beauty that other women spent hours in front of the mirror with hundreds of dollars in cosmetics to mimic.

"I'm in the doghouse at the moment," I smiled in response. "So, I'm working remotely today."

"It's a good look for you," she replied, taking in the slightly fitted muscle t-shirt removing the sweatshirt had revealed; her eyes lingered on my biceps before returning to me.

"Thanks," I smiled. "Can you point me to any news clippings from around the time Thomas Andrews died? I still need to get my library card, so I couldn't access anything online from my condo."

"I can," she said, "and I can also get your card, too. Just need your photo ID."

I flushed slightly. "I, uh, still have my Maine Driver's License."

"Oh," she laughed. "Well, then let's focus on the research first. Step this way, Detective."

I followed her around to a small room that had old-fashioned microfilm and microfiche readers along one wall, and research computer workstations on the other. Along the rear of the space were multiple aisles of movable bookshelves, stuffed full of small boxes. Pausing at the workstations, Beverly turned. "I can narrow down a bit if you tell me what you're looking for. As I said, Thomas Andrews is a popular subject around here, so I'm well versed in his history."

I nodded as I leaned against the chair. "All right. I need to know more about his estate, but I'm also interested in knowing if he won an Oscar."

Beverly smiled. "That last one is easy. It was for his most famous movie, *The Sinking of The Molly Brown*."

"Is that some sort of play on words?" I asked, thinking of the famed woman who'd survived the *Titanic*.

"No," she laughed. "It was a period piece with pirate ships, exotic tropical islands and buried hidden treasure. There was enough swashbuckling that he swept Best Picture, Best Director and Best Art Direction, though he missed out on Best Score."

Arching an eyebrow at her, I asked: "Do you have the movie here?"

"Yes," she replied, bemused, "but it's perennially checked out."

"Really?" I asked, a bit astonished. "When was it made?"

"Forty-eight or forty-nine, I think. Certainly one of the last movies to come out of the classic studio system."

"And it's still popular? It still stands up to the test of time?"

"It does," she said. "In many ways, Thomas Andrews was ahead of the curve. He was making summer blockbusters decades before the studios discovered them. Again."

"I might have to get on the waiting list, then," I smiled. "Once I get my card."

"You might have better luck on one of the streaming services."

A thought struck me. "How tropical was the movie? Palm trees and sand? Or more specifically, where was the buried treasure?"

"Are you sure you want me to tell you?" she asked. "It kind of spoils the movie."

"Humor me."

Beverly sighed. "Well... it goes against my better judgement. But the short version is the long-dead pirate whose treasure is being sought happened on a cave hidden behind a waterfall on one of those lush jungles in the South Pacific somewhere. The main character cracks the hidden code on a special map that was bequeathed to him and in the final scenes of the movie, discovers the gold and riches left behind." She paused. "And gets the girl of his dreams, too; the girl, I might add, who helps the main character crack the code."

"That's pretty progressive for the Forties."

"It was indeed." Beverly paused again. "You know, that's made me think of something."

I waited as she looked into space for a moment.

"Let me go grab the official biography," she said. "I'll be right back."

"Okay," I replied to her receding form.

Not knowing how long she would be gone, I pulled out my laptop and claimed an empty space next to one of the research stations as my own. By the time she returned with a stack of books, I'd logged into the VPN for the station and had begun to re-scan the contracts Rosie had with her publisher; the financials for Lillianna were being retrieved from the cloud equivalent of cold storage and wouldn't be ready for thirty minutes.

"You said 'biography,'" I pointed out as she dumped the books beside me. "That sounded singular to me."

"Well, you know librarians. Why use one source when you can have ten instead." Pulling the top one off the stack, she flipped to a section she'd marked with an index card. "Here's what I was recalling," she said as she held it down to me.

I started reading where her finger was pointing.

One long standing rumor around the studio had always been that there was an alternative ending for *The Sinking of The Molly Brown*, one so provocative that the famous producer/director was forced to replace it with extensive reshoots on location at the last moment. The studio heads at the time were not pleased with his particular take on progressive politics, and felt his movie needed to be cleaved of such idiosyncrasies. Fortunately for them, the revised ending fit well with the original script and allowed the movie to continue on to becoming a multiple-Oscar winning feature.

This so-called "lost reel" has never turned up; though while not especially valuable, in recent years the current owners of the movie's copyright have considered re-releasing it with the alternative ending in what could only been seen by movie buffs as an unvarnished attempt to cash in on the name of a long dead but still well-regarded titan of the industry.

"Ouch," I said as I looked up.

"If you think about it, in this era when old movies are getting facelifts, this could be worth millions," she said. "The scuttlebutt here at the library is that Thomas buried it up at the mansion but died before telling anyone where it was."

"Was he the sort of man to do that?" I asked. "I don't really know much about him."

"This one--" she pointed to another, thicker tome labelled *Thomas Andrews: The Man Behind The Legend*, "has that sort of detail, but I would say, yes. While he did a lot philanthropically for the nascent Rancho Linda, he also planned on taking care of his heirs. But when he died, all that was left was the mansion and few investment accounts."

"What about his staff?"

"That I don't know," she said, "but you can find that in this book too."

"Okay," I replied. "One last thing, if you don't mind."

"Sure."

"Was there a magazine exposé on any renovations or improvements that were made to the mansion over the years? Specifically, in the period right after *Molly Brown*?"

"I can find out," she smiled. "That's the sort of thing we do around here, anyway."

"So it is," I laughed. "You've been extremely helpful – thank you."

"My pleasure," she replied. "Let me see what I can come up with."

Twenty-Two

Two cups of coffee from the Staff Lounge and several dozen magazine articles later, I finally found a knock off of one of those *Better Homes and Gardens* walk throughs penned by a local resident of Rancho Linda for a magazine I'd never heard of. Published about seven years before Thomas Andrews died, it was a glossy eight-page spread showing before-and-after shots of multiple areas of the mansion.

I wasn't exactly sure what I was looking for, to be honest, but having seen how empty the space was under the current owner, I had quite a bit of curiosity as to what it must have looked like during its heyday. I wasn't disappointed as I flipped the pages, for while it appeared Andrews continued to tinker with various rooms over the five decades he lived there, he seemed determined to retain that sense of grandeur a home for a titan from the Golden Age of Screen should have had.

Heavy, dark-toned furniture complimented light walls; flowers were everywhere, and much like the orchids I'd seen in the solarium, seemed to have been specifically chosen to complement whatever space they were in by color or shape. Many, according to the article, had been grown on the grounds, making me think the gardening staff had been much larger in those days. Massive oil paintings from the forties gradually were replaced by lighter watercolors painted by a star he'd known for years; shag carpet gave way to wood and then tile in some rooms, though the terrazzo in the foyer appeared to have been there from the beginning.

As times changed and his staff became fewer, the quarters for the servants gradually became more focused, and personal; one room became a photography studio (complete with a dark room) while another, the writing room I'd seen already. Apparently at the time of the article, he was in the middle of penning his memoirs, a book that had never come to fruition.

The final page was a full-color shot of the solarium. By that point, I'd seen plenty of photos of the great producer, from the very young ones when he'd broke into stardom at age twenty-seven to one of a stooped, greying nearly anonymous old man taken by paparazzi outside of the Walgreens in downtown Rancho Linda two months before he died. Here in the shot from the magazine, Thomas still looked relatively vibrant at ninety-one, his thinning hair gray, but those eyes full of intelligence and, maybe, a bit of humor. He was standing at the far end of the pool, next to the waterfall, and was evidently pointing out something to the journalist as the picture had been snapped.

Scanning the article again, there was no trace of what might have been said other than a parenthetical aside noting just how hot and humid it had been in the solarium. I could relate completely. Flipping through the photos a third, and then a fourth time, I was astounded at how warmly decorated the house was, and how appealing it felt. If I'd not known I was looking at a multi-million-dollar home, I could have convinced myself it was something just on the north side of middle class – excepting the solarium.

Setting aside the magazine, I made a mental note to look for signs of the renovation during my walk through later. Seeing the space filled with items seemed to knock some of the sense of despair out that I had felt on my first visit; Rosie's emptying of the home, while well intentioned, seemed to have created a barren, melancholy space.

Turning back to my computer, I shifted screens to review the probate filings for Thomas Andrews and thanked modern technology from saving me a trip to the county courthouse. Digging through dusty boxes of wills and other end-of-life documents had never been a favorited pastime of mine, so I was doubly thankful for the ability to mark up the documents virtually. Considering how much Thomas Andrews had been assumed to be worth, the documents laid bare his actual wealth was the mansion, its contents and a paltry half million in mutual funds. Considering he was close to nearing the century mark when he died, I supposed it said something that he *still* had that much in the bank.

Pretty much as Beverly had explained, the cash had gone to the grandkids, and the home to his eldest son – Chief Andrews' father. I knew from other documents he'd immediately put it on the market, though it had sold many, many multiples below market value to a then up-and-coming new author. My eyebrows had gone up when I'd finally tracked down the transaction, for there was no question Rosie bought it at a fire sale price.

My eyes fell to the stack of photocopied news articles spanning the fifty or so years Thomas had lived in Rancho Linda. They represented highlights of his time, ranging from the first article announcing the building of his mansion to his death notice decades later. In between were peppered the many philanthropic gifts he'd made to the town, including a new pool at the high school to replacing the landscaped median outside of City Hall. He'd even sponsored the Fourth of July fireworks from 1950 to 1962, though there was no mention of why he chose to stop that year.

I figured that was actually tactful good taste, for his wife of twenty years had passed in '63, after a two-year fight with cancer. All but one of the kids – a daughter – had been grown at the time, though I'd been unable to trace her movements beyond that year in the few hours I'd been at it. Beverly had given me a vague "she moved to the East Coast" answer when I'd asked, and for the moment, it was good enough for me.

Sitting back in the hard-edged chair, I tapped my fingers against the well-worn desk and cogitated. Despite the note that Lillianna had sent Chief Andrews, nothing I'd turned up so far hinted at any sort of scandal she might have witnessed and then felt compelled to stay silent about. Not that I could truly trust the glowing portraits that had been painted of the family over the years, but considering how consistent they had all been – by different authors and different outlets, no less – it was hard not to think there was a kernel of truth to them. Andrews and his family had genuinely been well liked benefactors to the growing Rancho Linda.

Punching at the computer again, I pulled up the ME's report from Andrews' death, reconfirming for myself yet again that he had drowned; the water in his lungs had chemically matched that of his pool, and without any other signs of foul play, seemed pretty cut and dried. It was possible someone had lured the nonagenarian into the water and held him down, but he'd been fully clothed at the time, making it seem more likely he'd stumbled in and not been able to get out. The photo from Walgreen's had shown a man for whom time had caught up; it was entirely plausible he'd not had the strength to pull himself out of the water.

It wouldn't be the first time a senior citizen had fallen and been unable to get help.

The investigation at the time seemed to support this view and had been fairly quick – though not Mark Freidman quick. They had taken four weeks to go through it by the book, more perhaps to satisfy the terms of the small life insurance policy he'd also had. Unless I found something in the solarium during my visit later that day, it was unlikely I'd be able to shed any light on the old case for my boss after all these years. But hope sprung eternal.

Glancing at my phone, I realized it was nearing the noon hour and decided I'd done enough damage for the day. Packing up all of the materials I'd made copies of, I slid the computer into my backpack and then carefully toted the massive stack of books and magazines out to the reference desk.

Beverly caught my approach and hurried around to take some of the stack from me. "All done?" she asked.

"For now, yeah," I replied as I slid the rest onto the desk. "Thanks a million for your help."

"It was useful, then?"

"Immensely."

"Do you want me to keep these handy? In case you need them again?"

I started to say no, and then paused. "Yeah, would you mind? I can call over if I find I won't."

"Not at all. I'll keep them here at the desk."

I smiled. "Well, thanks again. You may have helped me solve an old case."

She smiled wider. "We're a full-service library," she chuckled.

Twenty-Three

I was starting to worry about my eating habits as I swung through Panda Express on my way to the mansion; the research from the library had me feeling like I was tantalizingly close to seeing the whole case spread out in front of me, so I'd reluctantly given up my run at lunch so I could head directly to the mansion and begin an afternoon of sanctioned snooping.

Being the lunch hour, traffic was heavy but nowhere near the worst peak of rush hour, so I made excellent time and turned through the lion-flanked gates a bit after noon. Each time I visited, the massive house had palpably felt different to me; as I locked the SUV and walked to the doors again, that afternoon, it simply felt empty. And lonely.

Fishing through my pockets, I came up with the key Rosie had provided; with her housekeeper out until the weekend, I'd needed a way to get in. Looking at the key in my hand, it struck me as funny that it had clearly been made at a local hardware kiosk – Ace, if I was seeing the logo right. It seemed a bit ironic that a three-dollar blank now allowed access to a multimillion-dollar mansion.

Sliding it home, I twisted the key followed by the knob of one-half of the massive set of doors, then pushed my way into the foyer. I was met by stale air, something I'd not noted previously. Given she lived alone and spent the majority of her time in the solarium, I wondered if the air conditioning system had been disabled or, at the very least, turned to an unusually high temperature so it wouldn't run frequently. I was glad I'd left the sweatshirt in the SUV.

I hadn't noticed the first time I'd visited that the terrazzo tile had a thin vein of jade in it, offsetting the white. It was astoundingly gorgeous even in the filtered light coming through the partially drawn curtains. Taking a step forward, I considered how I wanted to handle my search. Given how much time had passed since Lillianna's death, and how much more since Thomas Andrews' demise, bringing in the full crime scene process seemed unlikely to net me anything. Unless I found something specific, though what *that* might be was still elusive.

Somehow, though, I knew I'd recognize it were I lucky enough to stumble upon it.

Methodically, I started from the front of the mansion and began to clear the rooms. My initial going was quick and easy, since save for the writing room, the solarium and the kitchen, the first floor was just as barren as Rosie had told me it would be. Hundreds of square feet of space were completely empty, making the mansion feel even larger – and lonelier – than before. I saved the solarium and writing room for later but did poke through every nook and cranny of the restaurant-industrial-preparation-sized kitchen. Aside from a reasonable number of items in the fridge and pantry for a woman living alone, the only oddity I turned up was seven gallons of rainbow sherbet in the freezer.

A small room off the pantry appeared to have once been the wine cellar; though not dusty from disuse, it had maybe fourteen bottles in racks built to store a hundred times that. Most were the venerable Two Buck Chuck variety from Trader Joes, though one outlier bottle had a label from a vineyard in Sonoma and was a vintage older than me. Closing that door led me to the garage, which had space for three cars but only housed the Oldsmobile I'd spied earlier, and one of those luggage carts you often see in hotels. The glint of the light against the brass had caught my attention – that and the otherwise empty nature of the space. I wondered if Rosie had used it to move some of the "stolen" items from the writing room to her car. It certainly seemed large enough to hold the television, at least.

Retracing my steps to the foyer, I climbed one side of the elegant staircase and started going through the rooms on the second floor. As with the first floor, most were empty; in its heyday, it appeared the mansion had been capable of sleeping a family of twelve, each with their own personal bathroom. Rosie had clearly taken over what was the original master suite, comprised of two adjacent rooms; the first was a small, comfortable living room space with a recliner, TV-dinner tray table, and a boxy tube television atop a small piece of furniture. I wasn't surprised to see it had rabbit ears, and when I turned it on, only seemed to get the local PBS station. However, it did make me wonder why she'd had a flat-screen television in the writing room; it was another loose end among many.

Massive bookcases stuffed to overflowing were on one wall, and the large windows opposite looking down across the valley gave a slightly better view than the one from the writing room. A small banquet beside the door to the bedroom had a cocktail setup, complete with an old-fashioned seltzer bottle and stainless-steel martini shaker. I went through the titles on the bookcase, even pulled a few down to flip through, but didn't encounter a clue of any sort dropping into my lap.

The bedroom space was half the size of the sitting room, with what looked to be a queen-sized bedframe. Sitting between the two windows was a traditional dresser with mirror; unsurprisingly, given how unpretentious Rosie was, other than a comb and cherry flavored Chapstick there wasn't much to see. Hesitating slightly, I pulled out the drawers and found what I expected; undergarments carefully folded and stored away in one set of drawers; socks, sweaters and other items in others. Nothing was hidden among the folds of fabric aside from bars of fragrant lavender soap.

Two other doors led to a walk-in closet and the full bath, respectively. The closet was only a quarter full, mostly of out-of-date power suits Rosie must have worn when she'd last been doing the rounds of publicity for her latest book. A tiny section had cubbyholes of the type used to store shoes; Rosie instead had filled them with swimsuits and sweatshirts. I found maybe three sets of sneakers, total, and two sets of high heels. For a millionaire, she didn't seem to be much of a clothes horse.

The bathroom had seen some renovations, though. As I entered, the pungent smell of chlorine filled the air, leading me to the deep jacuzzi tub humming to itself in one corner; a quick test with a finger confirmed it was heated and ready for use. There was a walk-in shower, tiled in granite, and small alcove for the toilet. Double sinks in a vanity below an ovoid-shaped mirror finished the space, all of it tied together with a gentle palette of pastels.

I sat on the edge of the jacuzzi and for a moment was tempted by the warmth of the water. Much like my days as a college student-athlete doing two-a-day workouts, I'd simply toweled down and then tossed warmups on over my swimsuit so I could maximize my time with Rosie at the hospital; as a side effect, I was suitably attired for a thorough, clue-seeking search of the jacuzzi. While I was certain Rosie would have approved of my use of her space, I knew it was a clear breach of protocol, and given my ill-informed dalliance with Mark, I was already batting a thousand.

Reluctantly I ran my hand through the inviting water one last time and sighed; there was no question I'd hunt down the jacuzzi at the condo's common area later and try to unwind a bit. Shaking off the water, I looked around the bathroom again. None of the spaces I'd been through seemed any bit out of the ordinary. Not that I had much experience with millionaires or their mansions.

No, that wasn't entirely true; for sixteen years, I had been part of a wealthy family, wanting for nothing. On that fateful day when they had disowned me, I'd fallen from Olympus with not even a silver spoon to my name; still, all those years as the sole child of a well-to-do-family had never happened in a place as grand as Rosie's mansion – either in its heyday or what it had become afterward.

It was, I thought, a completely different life. One that I didn't miss. At all.

Standing, I moved back through the bedroom and out into the hallway; trotting down the steps, my running sneakers squeaked a bit on the tile, reverberating through the space and accentuating how empty it was. I paused at the bottom of the steps to check my phone; there were no messages from the station demanding my presence elsewhere in Rancho Linda, nor had the hospital given me the go ahead to retrieve Rosie. Seeing there was nothing else on my schedule, I strode down the hallway to uncover whatever secrets the writing room might hold.

Twenty-Four

The writing room's space had been carefully laid out the first time I'd been in it; now, it bore the signs of my abrupt entrance in the form of plywood over the missing glass and general disarray from the efforts of the first responders who had pulled her from the brink of death just the prior morning. One of those thousand-dollar desk chairs was over in the corner, on its side; I carefully righted it and slid it to her desk before sitting down in it. The replacement computer was there and still on; tapping the keyboard, the flatscreen monitor lit up but prompted me for a password. Flipping over the keyboard, I found the requisite Post-It note and transcribed the password, granting myself access to her virtual desktop.

It wasn't very exciting, for as she'd repeatedly told me, it was disconnected from the outside world. Aside from a special program for publishing, it was pretty bare. Someone had even removed solitaire, making me wonder if her editor thought she was goofing off instead of writing. Flipping back to the word processor, I could see she already had something like three hundred pages complete in her latest work. I'd never read her books, but reviewing what was on the screen, I could see her style was elegant and accessible. It was easy to see why she was so popular, and I made a note to check out her earlier material from the library.

I scrounged through her drawers and found little of interest, then did the same for the books in the smaller bookcase. The file cabinets held an amazing assortment of materials, more than I had time to truly search through properly. Scanning through the drawers, the filing system reminded me of an old book I had read in grade school, *The Mixed-Up Files of Mrs. Basil E. Frankweiler*, for the indexing seemed to be something just as unique to Rosie. Still, the last file in the last drawer provided something interesting.

Under the heading of *Plan*, I found eight-by-ten photostats of the plans for the mansion. Clearly done in a world pre-photocopier, they were blue-white and had a faint odor to them I couldn't place. Pulling them out, I took them to the window for better light and started to flip through them. The bold lines showcased the spaces and properly labelled each of the rooms I had been through, though most had something pretentious like *South Sunset Room* or *Grand Dining Promenade*. Digging through them it became apparent the plans were for the original owner, Thomas Andrews, and fairly well represented how the mansion had been originally intended to be used.

There were some surprises.

On the second floor, one room was labelled *Nursery* and another, *Nanny*. I wondered what it had been like to grow up in that mansion, child of a famous movie producer; that Chief Andrews had gone into public service made me think the experience of *his* father may have affected him in ways subtle and not. Another space was labelled *Screening Room* and showed a projection booth and slanted flooring; I'd not seen that in my travels and wondered if Rosie had removed it or if Thomas himself had repurposed the area after he fell out of favor with Hollywood.

Most intriguing was a sketch of the solarium. It was incredibly detailed, including the winding stone path I'd already seen, placement of the pool, the plantings around it, and designs for the patio furniture. It was hard for me to fathom that the very items I'd been sitting upon, casually chatting with Rosie, had been designed back in the Forties specifically for that space. I wondered if the palm trees and ferns I saw earlier were the same as the ones planted originally, or carefully replaced updates to keep the space as close to the original concept as possible.

I started to put the file back into the folder when something struck me. Pulling it open again and flipping to the solarium, I peered more closely at the design. I couldn't put my finger on it, but something was off. I'd seen a similar sketch in the magazine article earlier, but my notes – and the copy of the article – were in the SUV. Maybe I was just getting a little fuzzy around the edges.

Or, maybe not.

Closing the drawer, I took the file with me and headed to the solarium. Once more the rush of humidity was overwhelming, and I felt myself begin to sweat in the steamy air; within moments, my muscle tee was sticking to me in places. Working my way down the stone pathway, I arrived at the centerpiece pool and stood at one end. The plans confirmed that it was indeed an Olympic-length fifty-meters end to end, though with the river rock waterfall at the far end, it felt less like a workout pool and more like a recreational one. Still, I checked the plan again, for having a pool built of that distance in the 1940s was... unusual. I'd not run across any reasoning for that particular size in my research at the library, though.

As with the jacuzzi, the water called out to me, more so perhaps as rivers of perspiration began to trickle down my face. The water looked so cool and inviting by comparison, and the way the waterfall was cascading over those roundish river rocks---

Holy shit.

A bolt of adrenaline shot through me, and I looked at the design again in my hand. It was for a pool – there was no notation for the cascading waterfall. The water feature had to have been added later. The tiny frisson of excitement I always got when I knew I was starting to pull a thread bubbled up, and I wondered if I should play a hunch.

What the hell, I thought.

I placed the file on the wicker couch and literally ran out of the solarium, down the hallway and out to my SUV; unlocking it, I pulled the door open to the backseat and dug through my swim backpack to come up with my goggles, and as an afterthought, my swim cap. Locking the SUV up, I ran back through the house, my sneakers squeaking again on the tile as I bolted through the space, caught up in my own excitement. Back in the solarium again, I stripped off my t-shirt and yanked down the wind pants, revealing my blue-and-white briefs from practice that morning. As I walked to the edge of the pool, I stuffed my ponytail into the rubber of the cap, pressed the goggles to my face, and then cleanly did a racing dive into the water.

Arms outstretched, I did a series of hard dolphin kicks underwater to bring me to the base of the waterfall; as I'd suspected, the rocks quite oddly went to the bottom of the pool along the centerline of the far wall, unnecessary for a purely decorative item. It did strike me as looking like something out of a movie – like, say, one where a secret treasure was hiding.

Behind a waterfall.

Treading water to stay in place, I looked over the rocks that were below the waterline, tracing them with my eyes, looking for – and finally finding – a pattern in how they were fitted against the wall.

Kicking to the surface, I gulped a lungful of air before diving under again, then carefully began pressing, pulling or otherwise attempting to shift any of the rocks. I had to repeat the surfacing maneuver twice before my fingers finally found a small hidden latch toward the bottom of the rock façade; at nearly eight feet deep, the pressure was intense but bearable. Pressing the button, a *click* reverberated through the water around me. I tried to tug, but was unable to move the rock; kicking for the surface again, I broke through to air and treaded water in place for a moment.

Taking a deep breath, I dove down once more, gripped the rock with both hands and planted a foot on either side of the façade. Using my feet as anchors, I pulled as hard as I could and was rewarded by seeing the hidden door I'd found swing to the left, releasing a massive bubble of air in the process. The motion sent me floating backwards, forcing me to flip and stroke forward to peer into the space I'd uncovered.

Lungs burning, and my vision colored by the green of my goggles, I could nonetheless see it was intended to be a vault of some kind; several shelves contained a wide array of items, all carefully wrapped in plastic against water exposure. Not everything was recognizable, but I saw at least one film canister and – if I wasn't mistaken – what looked like one of those Oscar statuettes. Unless I missed my guess, I'd found Thomas Andrews' personal safe deposit box, hiding in plain sight of anyone visiting him at the mansion. It was a clever homage to the movie that had been his signature achievement, though I did wonder at the wisdom of choosing to place it underwater.

I dolphin-kicked up to the surface again and bobbed for a minute, then dove down a final time, intending to close the vault until I could get the crime scene techs to properly remove the contents. But as I swam toward the door once more, it unexpectedly snapped shut much like one of those giant oysters. I reared back, inadvertently releasing most of my air supply in one giant bubble of shock. Whether from my movements around it or some other reason, I wasn't entirely sure; what I *was* sure of, though, was the tiny fragment of fabric that was now visible along the edge of the hidden aperture.

Ignoring the burning of my lungs, I swam closer, examining the triangular piece of... something... through my green-tinted lenses. Pulling at it confirmed it was lodged firmly in the door, but I was sure it hadn't been there originally. As I tugged at it again, the very mechanical sounds of a pump kicking in reverberated in the water around me, and the waterfall a few feet above me seemed to increase in intensity. Bowing to my need to breathe, I kicked for the surface and bobbed again in front of the water feature, which was indeed flowing as though it were affected by a flood of some sort.

Suddenly, I understood the air bubble that had appeared when I opened the vault, and found myself nodding into the surface of the water as the flow ebbed back to the normal fountain I'd come to know. An air-tight, water-tight, underwater storage locker hidden in plain sight. This grandparent of Chief Andrews was proving to be fascinating, and I was starting to think I knew what the fabric might be from, too. The library expedition was shaping up to have been very productive, indeed.

Diving slightly, I did a few strokes of fly to get to the edge and cleanly pulled myself out of the pool in an easy move borne of long experience. Rotating, I remained seated on the edge, legs in the cool water, and pushed my goggles up to my forehead. I was at an unusual angle, looking out across the side of the water feature and the fogged-up glass of the solarium, and realized the rocks were simply stacked up on each other without any sort of cement to hold them in place. Standing, I wandered over, dripping along the tile as I went, and saw that the pipes and pump for the water feature were, in fact, simply surrounded by free-standing rocks.

I knew this, for one entire section had slid away from the plumbing, exposing the mechanics. It wasn't visible from where Rosie normally sat, but I was still surprised she hadn't noticed it. Anyone getting within a few feet of it could easily see it had been knocked asunder, for it was clear someone had removed a keystone at some point.

A round keystone.

Shit.

Despite being soaked, I yanked my wind pants on and grabbed my sneakers, trying to use the t-shirt to dry off the worst of the water from my torso as I hurried out of the solarium – belatedly realizing my towel was out in the SUV. I knew I was trailing water behind me as I made my way back to the writing room, but I was on the scent now and needed to see it through.

The space was still in disarray, but this time I knew what I was looking for. Something that shouldn't have been there or in the garden outside. I finally found the medium-sized rounded river rock in the far corner of the room where I had dropped it after seeing Rosie's insensate form; kneeling beside it, dripping all over the carpet, I picked it up and rotated it. I'd need to see the crime scene photos again, but I was nearly certain I had located the murder weapon – and, possibly, solved a thirty-year-old cold case, too.

Twenty-Five

Chief Andrews wasn't a happy camper.

Still somewhat damp from my impromptu search, I was leaning up against my SUV trying to dry out in the slanting rays of the late afternoon sun, arms crossed and looking at the golden pavers of the driveway. While I'd not anticipated overt kudos for cracking the case, I'd neither anticipated an even *more* severe dressing down than the one I'd received after disclosing my relationship with Mark Freidman. I knew my face was flushed in embarrassment as he called me out in front of the crime scene techs that were hustling around us in and out of the mansion; I felt like a rookie fresh out of the academy.

"--no warrant! And the barest, thinnest probable cause I've seen in thirty years on the job---"

I slid my sunglasses down to cover my eyes and then made like I was keeping eye contact. In reality, I was miles away, trying to keep the investigative thread I'd begun to tug at alive in my mind. Desperately I wanted to micromanage the collection of artifacts from the small vault or dig back through the paperwork I'd gotten from the library. A hundred small things that needed to be wrapped up quickly so I could close the case. Or *cases*, as it happened. But Chief Andrews wasn't entirely wrong; I'd gone a little bit rogue and done it even after more-or-less being put on notice for my behavior. Not a positive trendline for a new member of the department with less than a week on payroll.

"---too close to this. I mean, Jesus! *Swimming* in the pool of a victim? I've never in my wildest---"

I'd actually made a third mistake by going directly to the Orange County Sheriff's Office of the Coroner and asking them to roll a Crime Scene team without passing it through the Chief first. In Windeport, I'd been empowered to do what needed to be done; Rancho Linda was more budget driven and paying for the techs to go over a mansion for a crime that was committed more than a month earlier wouldn't have been high on their list. Andrews had made that clear to me when he'd stormed into the solarium, interrupting my asking the tech to look for trace around the waterfall feature.

"Answer me!" Andrews thundered, yanking me out of my thoughts.

Unaware of what exactly his query had been, I opted for the failsafe. "It won't happen again, Chief," I replied as contritely as I could.

"It better not," he said, the color in his face emphasizing his displeasure. "God *damn!* You have been a handful and then some, Detective."

"My apologies, Chief."

"And on that note," he continued, lowering his voice and pulling me closer. "We have a bit of a problem. Well, technically, it's more of *your* problem."

"Mar--Detective Freidman?"

Andrews nodded. "He's filed a sexual harassment complaint against you with Human Resources. You have a meeting with them next Monday at nine." He lowered his voice further. "I shouldn't tell you this, but as a courtesy I was given a copy of the complaint. You should know he's alleging you've created a hostile work environment since arriving. Forcing him to do things he's not comfortable with."

I felt myself spluttering. "I--I *what*?"

"It's good you came to me last night, Vasily, but the truth is I can't weigh in on this. My replacement starts next month, so he'll be the one to make the call – based, unfortunately, purely on the outcome of the HR investigation."

I felt myself shaking, but in one sense wasn't surprised; the way he'd left the condo the prior evening had telegraphed that our private little war was far from over. Mark was clearly coming after me in a different way; oh, he was a smart one, for sure, and now I realized I'd been pitted against an expert manipulator of extraordinary talent. I wasn't easily seduced, but in the end, had been; somehow, he'd managed to get me to ignore my internal warning systems, ones I'd built up over years. It was infuriating to be outplayed like that, and I wondered if he thought trumping up a case with HR would apply enough pressure for me to subjugate myself to him in order to make the complaint go away.

How little he knew me.

"It's not true," I said icily. "It's just the opposite!"

"This is why we ban those sorts of relationships," the Chief said sadly. "And I *did* warn you."

Still shaking with anger, I nodded tightly. "Yeah. You did."

"Ah, shit," he said as he looked away.

I waited, feeling as though my future as detective was being decided in front of me. It was hard to watch as all of those years of effort were coming down to a stupid choice I'd made, but there it was. Folding my arms against my chest again, I braced myself as Chief Andrews seemed to settle on something.

"Damn it, you are a hell of an investigator, and the department can't afford to lose you." He turned back. "Solve this case – solve *both* of these cases, and it would be nearly impossible to fire you – especially since it was Detective Freidman's case originally. I might not have much clout, but I may still be able to put a bug in the ear of my replacement." He paused. "It might mean a demotion, though."

"Better than being drummed out," I replied.

"It won't be easy," he added. "The department is likely to be rather uncomfortable for a bit."

"I can handle it," I sighed. "Pretty much have since age sixteen."

Chief Andrews smiled at that. "I don't doubt it."

I looked over his shoulder to see the tech I'd been talking to at the pool appear at the double door; locating me, she hurried down the steps and paused next to us. "Detective? You were right."

Andrews looked between us. "About?"

The tech looked to me and I nodded before she continued. "Blood, sir. At least trace evidence of it, all around the water feature. It has been cleaned up, we assume with bleach, but we found something in an area beneath the plumbing where some had pooled."

The Chief looked at me. "I think that is where the housekeeper was killed, Chief. I suspect she was moved to prevent the discovery of the vault – for what reason, I'm unclear on at the moment, but I think I'm close to understanding that, too. And with the focus being on the computer, Detective Freidman never had the house properly searched."

Andrews shook his head. "It keeps coming back to that damn computer."

"It does," I smiled. "And I'm beginning to understand *why* as well."

Chief Andrews raised his eyebrows. "Do you want to share?"

"Not until I can prove it," I said. "For that, I need to do a bit more due diligence, part of which is to finish my review of the victim's financials. Then, I think, I need to have a nice, long chat with Dr. Frankenhoffer."

Twenty-Six

Much to Rosie's chagrin, out of an abundance of caution, her cardiologist decided to keep her in the hospital for another evening. I'd discovered this development when I'd dropped in fully anticipating the author would be chomping at the bit to get back home, only to find her still in the ICU, still hooked up to a battery of machines, and frowning at the tray of dinner that had been placed in front of her.

"I take it our plan has run aground," I said good naturedly as I leaned against the edge of the open glass door to her room. "What did you do? Piss off the head nurse?"

"Something like that," she groused. "Apparently my electrolytes or some such stupid thing are not in the right range, so I've been sentenced to another night of detention."

"Don't be so dramatic," I laughed as I came in and sat down on the edge of her bed in what was fast becoming my usual spot. "I'm sure they have good reason. And another night won't kill you."

"Says you," she moaned, but I could see a slight smile. Rosie wrinkled her nose. "Don't take this the wrong way, Vasily, but your shirt smells like it was drowned in a public pool."

I laughed. "That's fairly close," I replied, well aware that I was still attired as she had seen me earlier that day.

"That sounds like a story," she half smiled.

"I may have taken an unexpected swim earlier," I replied. "And I've not had time to change since."

Rosie looked me over a bit more closely. "You've not shaved in a few days, either," she observed. "Is everything okay?"

"Totally," I laughed airily. "I'm embracing the casual lifestyle here in Southern California."

"Right," she replied, clearly unconvinced. "What's really going on?"

"Nothing, honestly," I lied, knowing that any number of the things currently wrong in my life were worthy of their own novel in and of themselves. "It's just been a rather long day. Or days, I suppose."

"Ah," she replied, though I could tell I'd not been all that convincing.

Not truly wanting to get into my personal life with a subject of my investigation – I'd already crossed too many lines in less than a week – I decided it would be wise to cut my visit short. "Well, I guess I'll let you finish your dinner and watch *Jeopardy!*"

That made Rosie laugh. "Don't broad stroke it, young man," she said sternly, though I could see from her smile I'd managed to finally jolly her out of doldrums. "Not every old person watches Alex Trebek. Some of us prefer Pat Sajak."

"My mistake," I chuckled. "I'll be by in the morning."

She nodded, then added: "Thanks for thinking of me."

"Of course," I replied as I leaned in to give her a quick hug.

Rosie waved me off. "Vas, you need a shower."

"That I do," I laughed as I kissed her anyway and then made my way back to the SUV.

Wanting something a bit more solid than fast food for dinner, but not wanting to go back to the condo and cook, I detoured across the mid-evening rush hour traffic to fight my way to the diner. I'd not been there for anything other than breakfast since arriving in California but had spent enough time there to know they had a dinner menu. Unsurprisingly, the parking lot was full much like it was at my normal hour; I managed to score the final slot next to the dumpster, and then presented myself to the host for a seat.

I *was* surprised when I wound up in my usual booth, though, and even more surprised when, while trying to decide between the Shepard's Pie and meatloaf, a familiar voice appeared at the table.

"Hey."

I looked up and saw Drew, smiling slightly. He was deeply tanned, far darker than the base level he'd had before leaving to be with his boyfriend. "You look like you had a good time," I observed. "But aren't you back early?"

"I am," he nodded, and there was a slight trace of pain in his expression. "I wound up cutting it short and got back this noon. And just my luck: I picked up a double for my troubles."

"You are in for a long night," I replied, pausing, for as I looked at my new friend, I was unable to not apply some of my detective skills to him. Slowly, I nodded. "He took you on a romantic getaway just to break up, didn't he?"

Drew looked away and nodded tightly. "He... he's engaged to the 'other' guy back on the ship," he said softly. "This was his farewell tour with me."

"Ouch," I breathed, and my heart went out to him. "That's rough, man."

He tried to shrug with a half-smile. "I'll get over it. Not the first time I've been dumped," he said, but it was easy to see it was the first time it hurt. Badly.

"You want to talk about it?" I asked, holding my hand out to the open both. "Step into my office; my rates are reasonable, even if it is after five."

"Thank you, Doctor Vasily," He smiled. "But I'm on the clock."

"So you are," I said. "But the offer stands. When do you get off?"

"Double shift," he reminded me with a chuckle.

"Without a break? Between?"

Drew nodded. "I'm here until six tomorrow morning."

"Oh," I said, realizing work was actually some sort of therapy for him. "Well. Then I suppose the real question is whether I go for the meatloaf or something else."

"The prime rib is actually pretty good," Drew recommended. "Or the chili. We have a special recipe from the owner's cousin in Tucson. It'll blow a hole in your digestive track."

"Given the week I've had, let's go for the chili," I laughed as I handed him my menu. "But seriously – if you want to talk, call me and I'll meet you. Any time."

Drew smiled. "Let me get your order in."

"Okay," I smiled back, somehow knowing the call would never come.

Dinner still wound up being as uncomfortable as I'd originally expected. Drew came and went in a perfunctory way; not, perhaps, because of me, but more that he was moving through the phases of grief one experiences when a relationship falls apart. I'd had plenty of opportunities to experience it myself, and to be brutally honest, it never gets any fucking easier. I paid the bill, left a favorable tip and continued on toward home.

As I pulled into the garage, I took an extra lap around the visitor parking to ensure the mustang wasn't there; once burned, as they say, twice shy. I had no desire to be surprised again by my new nemesis, knowing now how he felt the victim. Parking the SUV in my spot, I sat in the driver's seat for a few long moments as the engine slowly cooled down, still not particularly wanting to go back upstairs. I'd investigated my share of sex crimes over the years and knew how it often rocked the victim to their core. It wasn't hard to recognize the signs in myself, either; the wariness, the fear of returning to the place where it happened. The fact Mark hadn't been able to complete the final act didn't lessen the impact that more than just my private life had been violated.

Home now felt foreign. And I'd only been there for a week.

Trying to shake it off, I grabbed my things and made my way up to the condo. I didn't realize I'd had my sidearm in my hand until my condo door was closed and locked behind me. It had been in the locked safe of the SUV the prior evening, a mistake that I planned never to make again. I didn't know what it said that I had no recollection of removing the Glock from said safe before getting into the elevator that evening.

Sliding the gun onto the nightstand in the bedroom, I returned to my kitchen and pulled out the last of my supply of Samuel Adams. Popping off the cap, I took a long drag of the bitter lager, and wandered to the window in the living room. The sun had gone down already, and in the distance, the lights on the castle at Disneyland had come up, bathing the structure in pastel hues that emphasized the fairy tale aspects of the construction. The Matterhorn was alive as well, glowing in white and purple; I'd been to the park so many times as a kid that I could hear in my head the way the wind whistled through the faux caverns, and the piped-in howls of the Abominable Snowman. After the nasty surprise of my last visit, I wasn't inclined to drive up again. But maybe in a few weeks.

Or not. I guess everything had to change over time. Wasn't that the entire point of this California escapade of mine, anyway? Sipping my beer, I shook my head, for I was starting to wonder; Sean continued to be in my thoughts despite my best efforts.

Turning, I considered my backpack and the full night of work it represented as it lay against the breakfast bar. I suspected I knew what I was going to find as I dug through the finances of Lillianna, but it had been a long day; sniffing an armpit, I decided it could wait a little longer and padded into my master bath for a long overdue shower. The hot water did a bit to revive me; a steaming cup of coffee did the rest, though it was not usually my preferred chaser after a decent bottle of beer.

Comfortably attired in my sleeping pants and an old anime t-shirt, I settled back in at the breakfast bar and pulled everything out. While the laptop logged into the department VPN, I took a moment to re-read the letter Lillianna had sent Chief Andrews. Checking the time on my phone, I took a chance and called the Chief.

He picked up on the first ring. "Detective? What's wrong?"

"Nothing, Chief. My apologies for calling out of the blue; do you have a moment?"

"I do," he said. "I was just getting a cocktail ready for the second half of Thursday Night Football."

"Who's playing?"

"No one that doesn't need a strong dose of alcohol to watch," he chuckled. "What's on your mind?"

"The letter from Lillianna."

There was a pause. "Ah," he said, and I heard him close a door. "I wondered if you'd want to know more about it."

"How well did you know her? I'm going out on a limb here and assuming you spent a bit of time at the mansion as a kid."

Andrews chuckled lightly. "Some. Father wasn't as close to my grandfather as my aunt was."

"Growing up as a child of privilege sometimes creates friction," I said, knowing a bit about that myself. "What sort of issues did he have with Thomas?"

"About what you would expect," the Chief replied. "Living under the shadow of my grandfather put an immense amount of pressure on him; not only was he the firstborn son of a famous movie producer, but he was also heir to the scion of Rancho Linda. It drove him away from Rancho Linda and into the Peace Corps the moment he was eligible to join. Dad told me later that it had infuriated my grandfather, for he'd carefully scripted out his son's life, one that would have him following the same path through Hollywood." Andrews sighed. "Problem was, the script was dated; by the late 1950s, the studio system had begun to crumble; Dad could see the writing on the wall in the 1960s and had no desire to go down with the ship."

"That created a split?"

"'Split' is kind. More like a massive cleaving of an iceberg from a glacier; the waves reverberated for years. But Dad was right. When he returned from his stint in Central America, Granddad was out, the product of a studio merger that suddenly had too many star producers and not enough projects to go around."

"So, he stayed away, even after that?"

"Oh yeah. I *maybe* went to the mansion once a year – the dutiful visit on Christmas, but never for longer than the time it took to take a photo, exchange gifts and get out of there."

"No fond memories of running up and down the staircase? Or swimming in the pool?"

"None," he laughed. "I didn't even *know* about the pool until the day grandfather died. I was part of the LAPD at that point and got pulled out of a departmental meeting to be told about it; I drove down shortly after and found my Dad waiting outside. He'd had to identify the body for the coroner."

Looking at the probate filing, I tapped my finger on the countertop. "I know the rest from there – though I'm still a bit surprised at how quickly the mansion was put on the market."

"You've seen his finances," Andrews replied. "We had no idea how little he actually had on hand when he died; Granddad managed to do a lot of good in this community, but it drained him financially. Dad was getting ready to retire himself at that point and had no need for a house that big; I had two kids myself, but they were already college bound. And none of us could afford the estate taxes or the property taxes. So, it was kind of an easy decision." He laughed. "But Granddad helped one last time – I have a doctor and a dentist in the family, thanks to his timely departure."

"I obviously don't know him well, but that sounds like something he would have appreciated."

There was a long pause. "Yeah, I think he would have."

I looked at the letter and realized Andrews had done an expert job of moving away from my original question. "Lillianna mentions closure in what she sent you," I said. "What is it that the family – your family – needed to know?"

I heard him circle some ice in a glass. "It was a long time ago now," he said, "and more my father than any other member of the family."

"Okay."

"It's the darndest thing," Andrews said after a long, long pause. I got the sense I was stirring up something that he'd packed up in a small box that he was just now pulling back the tape on. "Despite all of the hard feelings, he was never convinced his death was an accident."

Twenty-Seven

I was glad that Chief Andrews couldn't see my face. "In what way?" I asked, feeling like another piece of the puzzle was rotating a bit, and almost ready to be pressed home.

Andrews sighed. "Nearly from the moment they pulled my grandfather from the water, Dad suspected some sort of foul play had taken place. For the first time that I could recall, he leaned into his standing in the community as the Son of Thomas Andrews and forced the police chief at the time to open an investigation."

"I read the file," I said. "The process was fairly quick, but pretty thorough."

"It was. Still, dad wasn't convinced that Grandad's death had been an accident; he spent years formally or informally digging into it, trying to find the truth. My aunt thought he was nuts, given how old grandfather was; she figured he'd just lost his footing and fell in. Toward the end, Granddad *had* become a bit frail, a tiny bit unsteady on his feet; it was entirely plausible that he'd just slipped."

"That seemed to be the Medical Examiner's read on it," I said, nodding even though Chief Andrews couldn't see me. "The staff said your grandfather hadn't had a visitor in months."

"He'd pulled back from society after he turned ninety," Andrews said, the ice cubes clinking in his glass again. I could tell he'd lowered the volume of his tumbler somewhat and suddenly found myself wanting another beer myself. "And the staff had shrunk quite a bit by that point, too. He was down to four I think: the chef, the housekeeper, a gardener and his driver."

"Save for the gardener," I said, flipping to the old file on my laptop, "the rest were there the day he died and confirmed he'd been alone in the solarium. I still don't see anything nefarious."

The Chief blew out a breath. "Dad thought the staff either saw it happen; or, if they didn't *see* him fall in, they found him shortly afterward but still *let* it happen, though for what reason he was never able to divine. He had them investigated up to the hilt and got nowhere. Not one of them saw anything despite the entire staff being on duty that night."

"Forgive me for being frank, but what would the staff have to gain from killing your grandfather?"

"That would be the million-dollar question," Andrews chuckled. "Even though it wasn't in the will, Granddad had created several investment accounts for his servants; for the most part they were rather well taken care of. Pensions and healthcare – better than what I have now, actually."

"That could be motive, if those funds were only accessible after he passed."

"True," Andrews concurred. "But they were all vested immediately when he created the accounts for them about six years before he died. They were eligible to access them as soon as they left his employment."

"So, pushing him into the pool netted them nothing," I observed.

"Exactly. And they were incredibly loyal to my Grandfather; his driver was the oldest of the lot and retired after his passing. The rest went to work for the new owner of the mansion; Lillianna was the youngest and outlived the rest of them by a decade."

"Still, Lillianna's note would indicate that she knew something. I don't buy they watched him slip and fall and did nothing, if they were as loyal as you say."

"Me either," he agreed. "Which made me think it was something else." Andrews paused. "You know, I crawled all over that solarium for my father – I have to say, none of us saw what was hiding in plain sight. What tipped you off?"

"I heard about his most successful movie--"

"Ah, *Molly Brown*."

"Exactly. And to be honest, it wasn't until I came across the original plans for the mansion and realized the waterfall wasn't part of the pool when it was built that I started to put the pieces together. I will say, having an underwater safe seems a bit odd. I can't see your grandfather diving down when he wanted to visit with his Oscar."

Andrews was silent. "Unless it wasn't underwater all the time," he mused. "God *damn*!" he said softly.

Feeling a little lost, I asked: "I don't follow."

"Do you still have the keys to the mansion?" he asked.

"I do," I said.

"Meet me there. Bring the plans to the house with you; I'm leaving now."

"Uh, sure, Chief," I said, looking down at my Chat Noir sleeping pants and wondering what I had missed.

Changing into a clean set of warmups, I grabbed my backpack and service weapon, then sailed out of the condo to meet my boss. As late as it had become, traffic in Rancho Linda was light, and I made excellent time driving up from Anaheim to the mansion. Chief Andrews was standing next to his unmarked in jeans and a sweater and nodded as I approached.

"Did I miss something?" I asked, arching an eyebrow as I used the light from my iPhone to insert the key into the door.

"More like you asked the right questions to make me realize *I'd* missed something," he said cryptically.

I sighed. "You are *exactly* like my last boss. He used to see something but would wait until he could prove it to tell me."

"Comes with the title of *Chief*, Detective," he laughed as I opened the door and he followed me in.

We made our way to the fogged door of the solarium and then entered the space; I'd planned ahead and was only wearing a muscle tee. Chief Andrews immediately pushed the sleeves of his knit sweater up as he was hit with the suffocating humidity of the space, and tiny beads of sweat appeared on his brow. I was somewhat surprised to find how well done the landscape lighting was in the solarium; I'd not noticed the tiny Chinese lanterns every few feet along the pathway to the pool, nor the faux tiki torches that were flickering with an LED flame. The towering palm trees were tastefully underlit with floods, and as we came into the clearing, I could see the underwater lights were on in the pool, giving it an almost ethereal blue/green glow.

Andrews wasted no effort and moved directly to the far end of the pool, standing fairly close to where the rocks had come undone and slid away from the plumbing for the waterfall. He pulled a pair of exam gloves out of his pocket and, after sliding them on with a snap, leaned down on a knee to peer into the space. Following his lead, I had just finished gloving up myself when I saw him nod and wave me over.

"Damn," he said as he leaned back on his haunches, letting me slide in beside him. "See that?" he asked, pointing to something.

I leaned down and, in the dim light, trained my iPhone flashlight on the spot he indicated. A small dial, almost the same shape and size as one you would find on a timed jacuzzi was embedded inside another rock that had been cemented to the back of the waterfall. Sitting back, I could see that the stones that had slid down and away from the plumbing could, if stacked properly, cover the timer dial, hiding it from anyone casually looking at the feature. In fact, as I lifted a stone, it occurred to me that the loose fitting of the rocks had been intentional – allowing someone to remove them in order to gain access to said dial when needed.

"Clever," I said, looking to Chief Andrews. "But I'm not sure I understand the relevance. The fountain seems to run constantly."

"Exactly," he nodded. "Do you have those plans?" he asked.

"Yes."

Andrews reached in and twisted the dial, which clicked repeatedly until he stopped. As we stood, I heard the same mechanics as before, only this time, the waterfall flow slowed to a trickle and then stopped. Following the Chief over to the couch and coffee table where I'd met with Rosie earlier, I pulled out the plans from my backpack, all the while wondering why Thomas Andrews had a hidden timer that turned off his waterfall. It wasn't like disabling the flow would make it easier to access--

"Hot damn," I said with a smile, the plans in one hand. "He didn't access the vault while it was underwater, did he?"

"I don't think so," the Chief replied with a smile.

Putting the plans on the table, Andrews flipped to the site plan on the final page, showing the mansion and the surrounding grounds. I looked it over upside down and waited for the Chief to see whatever it was I had missed. "What is it?" I asked after a moment, curiosity compelling me.

"There's no outbuilding by the solarium on this plan."

I looked at where he was pointing and nodded. I'd jogged past it earlier when I'd been looking for Rosie. "What is it hiding?"

"Storage tank would be my guess," he said, nodding toward the pool.

I looked over my shoulder and could see the water level had gone down considerably. "I understand pumping out the water to get to the safe," I said as I looked back. "But why store it? Why not just refill it again?"

Andrews laughed. "That would be expensive," he pointed out. "And like most rich people, I would imagine Thomas Andrews wanted to save when and where he could."

I nodded. "And when the timer runs out? It refills from the storage unit?"

"Exactly," he said. "Very clever."

I stood up and walked to the edge of the pool. The pump or pumps in use were extremely efficient, for the level had gone down amazingly quickly; it was now quite easy to see how Andrews could have likely descended the steps at the shallower end of the pool and then easily walk to the vault. "Even if only half of the water is pumped out, he'd be able to access the vault," I observed. "That's still a helluva lot of water to store for a brief period."

"I imagine he didn't do it very often."

"No," I replied, "but it certainly would be easier to get that door open. The staff would have had to have known about this," I said thoughtfully and paused, the final piece of the puzzle snapping into place.

I turned, a partial smile on my face. "I think your father might have been right, Chief."

"About what?"

"Some member of his staff watched him die. And if I'm not mistaken, they couldn't do a thing about it."

Andrews looked at me. "No shit. How?"

"If you don't mind missing the rest of the game, I think I can prove it. Along with the forensics from the safe." I smiled. "As long as you *also* don't mind me taking another swim."

Slowly he nodded. "I'll bite."

Glancing at the water level, now at least a third lower than before, I looked to him. "Stand over by the waterfall and film this with your phone, would you?" I asked. "In case this goes horrifically wrong."

"Detective--"

"Kidding on that last part," I said as I kicked off my sneakers and pulled my t-shirt over my head. I shucked out of my sweatpants and then slowly went down the steps into the water in my boxer briefs, trying not to shiver at the cold embrace of the water. "If I am right," I said as I waded toward the deeper end of the pool, "I think there is a glitch in the system."

Andrews had his phone up and walked along the edge, paralleling my progress. "Keep going," he said.

More than half of the water in the pool had been removed; still, there was a good four feet of it that went to just above my belly-button by the time I reached the vault. Most of the door was above water, and I reached up to find the button I'd located earlier. It clicked, and the door sprung open; a small trickle of water dribbled out, but it had otherwise remained dry from being opened earlier by the techs. Seeing the shelves bare was a little odd.

As I examined the interior, there was a loud *clunk* noise and the whirring of the pump machinery ceased.

"How much time is left on the timer?" I asked, the water lapping around my midsection.

Andrews bent down in front of me. "Assuming the tick-marks are in one-minute intervals, maybe ten minutes?"

I nodded. "So, about ten minutes to drain the pool," I mused, "and about ten minutes to get in and do whatever you want with the safe. Then the process reverses."

"That's a little more than the average amount of time someone takes with a safe deposit box," Andrews said, then added at my raised eyebrow, "We have stats for that."

"I'm sure we---"

The rest of my reply was literally drowned out, for there was another loud *clunk* followed by the fountain immediately starting back up. A massive wave of water crashed down over me, slamming my body against the still-open door to the vault. It clicked shut with a finality, and it took significant effort to push myself out from beneath the deluge. As the water quickly began to rise around me, I flipped into a crawl and pulled myself out of the deep end.

Andrews met me at the top of the stairs. “Well, shit,” he said.

“But I need the forensics---”

“I’ll call the lab on my way back home,” he said. “You’ll have it in the morning.”

Twenty-Eight

Rosie was cleared to return home the following afternoon; I'd suspected as much after my morning visit with her (and a quick chat with the duty nurse) and was already in her room when the final paperwork appeared. Though she'd not been especially pale when she'd been admitted, her color was definitely closer to what it had been prior; certainly, her steps out to my waiting SUV were confident, if not a bit slower than normal.

Pulling the Police Prerogative card, I'd parked in the red zone outside the main entrance.

"Isn't this illegal?" she asked with a smile as I helped her into the passenger seat.

"For mere mortals, yes," I laughed. "Think of this as a VIP experience."

"Ah," she replied as I closed the door and went around to my side.

"Are you hungry?" I asked as I started up the SUV. "I can swing through McDonald's if you still want that Egg McMuffin."

"Now you're talking," she said.

Chuckling, I pulled into the late evening rush hour traffic and headed toward her house on a hill. I'd already scoped out a McDonald's that was on the correct side of the street (these things are important in California, given traffic flows), and somewhere close to seven, pulled up in front of her mansion. As much as I loved McDonald's myself, I knew the sour odor of grease would fill the SUV for a day or so and rolled the windows down a bit to try and get the worst of it cleared.

Unsurprisingly, Rosie insisted on inviting me in, and predictably brought me out to the solarium. I'd half expected it, actually, and had staged a slew of documents on the small coffee table by her favorite wicker couch before heading to the hospital to retrieve her. I was thankful they were only copies, since it was clear the humidity was already starting to curl them around the edges; but they were mainly there as a prop. Seeing the stack gave her pause, and she looked to me.

"What's that?"

"Things to talk about," I said cheerfully as I settled in on the seat I'd used before. "Sit," I encouraged as I unpacked my Quarter Pounder and a large container of French fries.

Considering me warily, she did, and pulled out her McMuffin from the brown paper bag. "This feels staged a bit," she observed.

"It is," I replied, leaning back and closing my eyes as I bit into the first QP with cheese I'd had since leaving Portland. It wasn't as good as the In-N-Out burgers I'd been dining on, but it was a close second. Opening my eyes, I watched as the landscape lighting began to come on around us in the solarium; even the lights within the pool slowly burned into existence. I thought again how impressively done the effort had been, especially given how there was enough ambient illumination that I could see Rosie clearly *and* read the paperwork in the files in front of me, if I'd not already committed them to memory.

I somewhat impolitely wolfed down my burger, realizing belatedly I'd not eaten lunch again. Picking up the red container of fries, I tried to pace myself and munched through it fry by fry. "So, I need to apologize. My unexpected swim was right here in this pool."

Rosie paused mid-bite of her muffin, looked at me, then to the pool, and back again. "Really? Why?"

"I'll get to that in a moment," I said. "Something you said to me during my first visit has stuck with me, to the point that it shaped some parts of my investigation."

"Oh? What did I say?"

"You told me Thomas Andrews had drowned in your pool."

"That's right," she said.

"And that Lillianna was on his staff at the time."

"Also true," she nodded.

"Did you find her body here?" I asked casually, slipping in the question as I munched on a fry. "Or, more specifically, over by the waterfall?"

Rosie's mouth dropped open. "How on earth..." she started before regrouping.

"We found her blood in a spot you wouldn't have been able to clean," I replied.

There was a long, uncomfortable pause that stretched nearly a full minute. I continued to eat my French fries, genial expression on my face. I could see Rosie was turning something over in her mind, and at length finally decided to speak.

"I didn't kill her," Rosie said quietly. "You have to believe me."

"I do," I said. "Although it's conjecture at this point, I think she slipped trying to open Thomas Andrews' secret vault." I ate another fry. "She sent a letter to Chief Andrews telling him she wanted to 'come clean,' and though we don't know exactly *what* she wanted to say, we are working under the assumption that she saw your visit to Saint Lucie as a chance to make sure the vault was still operational. And, possibly, show it to the Chief."

"Wait – *what* vault?"

Using a fry, I pointed to the water feature. "By our calculations, several million dollars of personal effects had been stashed in a small space below that waterfall," I explained. "You didn't know?"

Rosie's expression backed up her words. "No."

"Seems he put it in after his movie that won the Oscar," I explained.

"Chief Andrews didn't get the letter until after Lillianna was found dead, so we'll never know *what* she intended to tell him. But we are reasonably certain it was about the vault."

"I... I don't know what to say," she said, glancing over to the water feature. "All this time..."

"While I think I understand *why* you moved her, I'm a bit unclear how the rock that killed her wound up in your Zen garden."

"Ah. It's not a Zen garden," Rosie smiled slightly as she sighed. "I didn't realize it was *the* rock; that was just dumb luck. I needed something that could both break the window and appear to have killed her – to support my 'thief' narrative," she explained.

"You did move her, then."

"Yes," she nodded. "It wasn't easy, but fortunately she'd left the luggage carrier in the garage from when we'd loaded up the goods to take to Saint Lucie. I wheeled that sucker in here and loaded her into it." She sighed. "Despite her diminutive stature, it took me quite a bit to lift her into it. I'm still in fair shape, but it took me nearly thirty minutes to lug poor Lillianna over there."

I nodded, annoyed anew that Mark had never done a proper search of the grounds.

Rosie looked at me. "Most of what I told you was true; she *did* help me load up the car, and when I returned, she wasn't waiting for me. I searched the house and found her, face up, over there by the waterfall. It was clear she'd been dead for a day or so, but I couldn't fathom why she was in here."

"Why?"

"She'd told me some years earlier about finding Thomas floating in the pool. I might have mentioned that earlier."

"You did. Why did you move her?"

"To be honest? I think I thought it would help sell the theft of my computer," she said sadly. "It was a horrible thing to do to someone who'd served me loyally for years, but I guess I panicked." She looked away again. "After getting her properly displayed, I spent considerable amount of time cleaning up here and the trail I'd left to the writing room. Given how long she'd been dead, I didn't think another few hours more would make a difference."

"Probably not," I nodded, though I'd need to check the forensics again. "And then?"

"Then I called 9-1-1."

I nodded. "Well, the good news is the most I can charge you with is altering evidence," I said. "And filing a false police report."

"I see," she said, half of her Egg McMuffin in her hand, uneaten and presumably quite cold. "What am I looking at?"

"Both are misdemeanors," I said as I fished through the paperwork and handed her a ticket. "Fifteen hundred dollar fine, payable to the City of Rancho Linda."

Rosie looked at the ticket in her hand and I watched as a slow smile appeared. "That seems extraordinarily lenient."

"I'm not your publisher," I reminded her. "*We* may have let you off easily..."

"True," she frowned. "Well, I can deal with that."

"Good," I replied as I started to pack up my paperwork.

"Did Lillianna know how Thomas died?" Rosie asked after a moment.

"Yes," I nodded. "Or I suspect *strongly* she did. My best guess from the forensics is that Thomas – for whatever reason – drowned while trying to access the vault. She and the other staff members found him, but too late to do anything."

"They hid what happened?"

"I think so."

"Why?"

I shrugged. "Any number of reasons. Protect his legacy? Give him a more dignified ending? Preserve the secret of the safe?"

"That last one," Rosie said. "Why didn't they tell the family?"

"That is one mystery I don't have the answer to," I replied. "Probably the most basic reason, though. There was a falling out between the kids and Thomas. He felt betrayed by their life choices, and I'm sure the staff took the same view as their boss."

"But thirty years..." Rosie breathed. "That's a long time to bear a grudge."

Having some personal experience in that area, I smiled thinly. "Not for some people."

"Wow," she said softly, then looked at the pool again. "You said Thomas was trying to access his vault?" she asked.

"Yes," I replied.

"And he somehow drowned in the process?"

"That's right – we think the door to the vault malfunctioned and trapped him."

"Why do you think he was going to his safe?" she asked.

"Honestly? That's kind of bugged me to no end," I admitted. "Given his age, getting down into that pool just to open the vault would have been risky, even given how the pool drains."

"It *drains*?" Rosie exclaimed. "Man, the real estate agent I used didn't disclose *squat*."

"They might not have known," I replied. "It's not like it's part of the plans for this place; *I* didn't even find it until I took an unsanctioned swim."

"Good point."

I sighed. "Like I said earlier, what we found in the vault was definitely valuable, but without any remaining staff members to ask, it's hard to know if anything is missing." I glanced over my shoulder at the shimmering water. The underwater lights made the water seem to glow, which was strangely ethereal; the effect was heightened by the occasional bubble burbling up from the bottom courtesy of the filtration system. "I almost—"

The answer hit me with a near physicality, causing me to flinch. Rosie caught the movement and partially stood. "Vasily? Are you okay?"

"Yes, yes," I waved her back down to her chair. "Sorry. I think I just experienced one of those epiphanies people talk about."

"Oh? Mind sharing?"

I smiled slightly. "It just occurred to me that accidents often cover a lot of sins."

"What is that supposed to—" Rosie started to ask before her eyes went wide. "Shit. That's what Lillianna was going to give Chief Andrews, wasn't it? The knowledge that his grandfather took his own life?"

"Who knows?" I smiled a bit as I stood to go. "That's the trouble with cold cases. It's likely to be one answer we'll never find out."

Twenty-Nine

Monday turned out to be a really, really lousy day.

The weekend had been anything but; the half-dozen boxes I'd packed and shipped to California had arrived Friday, so most of Saturday was spent unpacking the rest of my personal items, completing the process of feathering my nest. My Camaro was still a few days away; as much as I appreciated having the department vehicle, I was seriously looking forward to having my own wheels. I knew I'd finally moved in when the framed shadowbox containing my Gold Medal went up in the bedroom; it was the final item I had packed from when I was living in the apartment over the pharmacy, so seeing it on the wall again felt like I'd finally settled into my new life. Somewhat.

Sunday morning, I spent at the beach with Drew, ostensibly surfing but in reality, helping him get over the upending of his relationship. It felt a bit self-serving on my part, for a not insignificant part of me was hoping I'd be able to fill the void for him on a somewhat permanent basis. I figured the fact that I'd woken up with my arms around him that morning was a reasonably good start in that direction.

Breakfast followed practice, and we parted ways in the parking lot with a promise to connect for drinks after I got off work. I harbored no illusions that my meeting with Human Resources would be pleasant. What I'd not counted on was the chill from my colleagues when I entered the station a bit before seven; despite being at a quarter of capacity, it felt as though all of them had suddenly decided to appear.

The feeling of unease continued into the locker room. I'd fallen into the habit of showering at the station after practice, and as I unlocked my locker to retrieve my shower gel and shampoo, I realized the two patrol officers that had been in the space ahead of me had stopped talking. Peering around the door, I could see they were hurriedly throwing on their uniforms, almost as if the space was suddenly on fire. Shaking my head, I disrobed and tied my towel about my waist, then started toward the showers.

A third patrol officer that I knew used the weight room prior to his day shift was already in the space, and as I hung my towel and went to the showerhead in the far corner, I heard him turn the water off. Now beginning to see a pattern, I turned as I reached for my controls.

"It's not like I have a virus," I called after his retreating form.

My eyebrows went up at his rather rude hand gesture.

By the time I'd put my hair up and locked my gear, I was utterly alone in the cavernous locker room. The space was usually bustling at that hour of the day, so the message was clear: I had become a pariah, one to be avoided if at all possible. Pushing out the door to the hallway, I wondered as I walked toward my cubicle just how much damage my reputation had taken courtesy of Mark; you didn't need to be a detective to deduce he'd spent the weekend ramping up a whisper campaign against me.

Unsurprisingly, his desk was bare when I dropped my gear. I knew Chief Andrews had planned on separating us, though it was unusual that the person with more seniority had been moved. My guess was the Chief was trying to ameliorate the coming discipline action, given how well I'd handled the cases.

I'd barely sat down when my phone buzzed. "Morning, Chief."

"Detective, this is Chief Gilbert. My office, please."

"Chief?" I asked, representing more than one question.

"Now, please."

As I hung up, I confirmed the call had come from Chief Andrews' line and made the assumption that Chief Gilbert was his planned replacement. We had all been scheduled for a two-hour one-on-one with the incoming Chief so he could come up to speed on the work of the department, but mine had been scheduled toward the end of the December owing to my own recent hire. Grabbing my notebook, I wondered as I hurried toward his office if that would help or hurt me. A knot of dread had lodged itself in my gut, though, and it became a full-on acid wash when I saw Gilbert sitting behind Andrew's desk. A red-tinged folder sat in the center of the blotter, unopened, though I could see my name and employee number on the tab.

"Sit," he said as I entered.

"Sir?" I asked as I took one of the visitor chairs. Based on his severe expression, the formality seemed necessary. "I was under the impression that you were starting in the new year."

"We've had to move up the timeline a bit," he said. "Chief Andrews is... ill. He will not be returning to work. Effective today, I am the Acting Chief, which will carry me through until my posting formally begins in January. I'll be shuttling between here and my current gig for a bit."

"What happened to the Chief?"

"Obviously, I can't disclose much. But the family has allowed me to pass on he is recovering from an emergency triple-bypass, after suffering a massive heart attack on Sunday. I'd prefer that this not go further," he added, reminding me with a sharp glance of our rather strict personnel policies.

"Of course, sir."

"I've read the complaint from Detective Freidman," he said. "I'm rather annoyed that it was brought to my attention almost as soon as I arrived. This is a helluva situation for me to deal with on top of everything else."

I decided just nodding would be easier.

"You are meeting with Human Resources this morning?"

"Yes."

"I'm not gonna sugarcoat it. Fraternizing with a fellow officer is against policy. If you thought you could pull it off because it was a same-sex relationship--"

"Never crossed my mind, sir."

"--clearly you blew that. Under normal circumstances, I'd have your badge and that would be that."

I nodded.

"However, the fact that you managed to close two cases, and put a coda on a third cold one tells me you are an asset this department cannot afford to lose. I've not read your file – hell, I've not had a chance to read *anybody's* file – but if you can do that level of work in one week, I need you right where you are and not out on unemployment." He looked at me, hard. "I'm reducing you two grades, with a pay cut to match. If you can prove to me that this was a one-time thing, I'll restore you a grade next summer, and another in the fall."

My eyes bugged out. "Sir! That's... that's less than I made as a rookie in Maine!" I exclaimed, shaking slightly. "And it's not justified! The allegations are spurious at best!"

"It doesn't matter," Gilbert said pointedly. "Whether you harassed him, or he harassed you, the fact remains that *both* of you played fast and loose with the expectations of the department. Disciplinary action was inevitable from the moment this became an action item for me."

"Chief," I said, my anger barely under control, "I relocated *specifically* for the role I was hired into. Stepping me back two grades over an unproven *allegation* is--"

"My decision is final," he said abruptly as he pulled the file from the desk and slid it into a drawer. "HR will give you the particulars, but the short version is you'll have a week of unpaid leave before you resume your duties. You'll also be assigned a supervisory partner for the next quarter until I decide you've worked your way out of the doghouse."

"With all due respect--"

"Am I understood?"

I wanted more than anything to explain to him how I viewed the insanity of his actions, and very nearly called up the video on my iPhone to help make my case. But as I saw the steely determination in the eyes of my new boss, the safer political play appeared to be to take it on the chin and survive to fight another day.

"Yes, Chief," I said quietly.

"Good," Gilbert nodded curtly. "Look, I know this seems rough. If it helps, Detective Freidman has also received a suspension and a double grade reduction." He looked at me. "Take this next week and decide whether being a member of Law Enforcement is truly what you want. And then come back and convince me not to dump your sorry ass on the pavement."

Quietly furious, and certain Gilbert could see it, I simply nodded to him and stood.

"Dismissed," he said to my unspoken question.

It stung as I returned to my desk and shoved my laptop into my backpack; the demotion meant I'd have barely enough for my lease, let alone any other living expenses. I'd be forced to dip into my savings just to make ends meet, and though that would last for a bit, it wasn't inexhaustible. I'd have to dig my way out of this demotion quickly or find a side gig. Or a new place, but housing in that price range came with a much, much longer commute.

Damn you, Mark Freidman. Damn you to Hell.

As I grabbed my stuff and deliberately made my way to the HR suite, I found within me the determination to right this wrong; somehow, I would find a way to work harder than everyone and turn this around. It was something I had learned working for Sean, and I saw no reason not to lean into that experience now. I'd already run circles around Mark; even with a *supervisor*, I was certain I'd be able to distinguish myself from my peers.

Such as they were.

Entering the rabbit warren of cubes for Human Resources, I stopped at the reception desk. “Vasily Korsokovach,” I said.

The young Hispanic receptionist looked at his calendar. “You’re two hours early,” he frowned. “Come back at your appointed time.”

“No,” I said, “I’m ready to do it now.”

“That’s not how--”

I leaned over the desk. “Look, sweet cheeks. I’m here *now*. Pull in whoever was supposed to do this thing and let’s get it over with. I need to get on with my life, and I’m sure they do, too.”

He narrowed his eyes in disapproval as he picked up the phone. “Mark said you were a drama queen.”

“Oh, honey,” I smiled. “You ain’t seen nothing yet.”

Epilogue

I didn't start out running the trail behind the Rancho Linda Police Department after work each night, but after several weeks of being on the shit list with Chief Gilbert – and dealing with the even *shittier* cases that were being handed to me – I'd begun to work well into each evening, intent on proving I was more than up to the task. Few dividends had developed from the effort quite yet, but it was still early days; I knew from past experience I was capable of out hustling *anyone* in the department, so it was just a matter of time before attitudes, however grudgingly, began to change. While there was a tiny bit of Pollyannaism baked into my assumptions, there was no doubt I was laser focused on regaining my original position.

Running after a long day at my desk had become a way to unwind before returning to my condo and putting in a few more hours prior to finally turning in. Considering I was still doing ten kilometers at lunch time, adding another ten every evening on top of still swimming a few thousand each morning *might* have been overdoing it a bit, but it seemed to be the only way to keep the stress of my situation from overwhelming me. With my budget temporarily curtailed by my demotion,

I'd had to get creative with ways to unplug. Running and swimming were big parts of that – and, for the most part, relatively inexpensive; while a night at the movies or trips to Disneyland were kind of out for a while, I'd recently discovered the live jazz performances on Friday evenings at *The Alternative Way* were free. It was irritating in the extreme to have to watch every penny, but I'd done it before. With luck, I wouldn't have to do it for too long this time around, but it was better to be cautious than not.

There were decorative lamps set every few yards along the pathway as it wound through the small, wooded area and then hugged the reservoir; though I had a head lamp, I'd never found that I needed it, and routinely left it in my locker. The trail was always fairly busy, too, full of people like me trying to get a workout in after work but before the rest of their evening continued. Walkers, runners, teens on rollerblades, parents with strollers – we all shared the nicely graded trail, though some seemed more intent on an *actual* workout than others.

I'm not sure *when* I realized I was being deliberately followed.

Once the late-evening runs had become part of my routine, it was easy to see the pattern that had developed; generally, the same people were out each night, and I met them at about the same place on the trail with nearly perfect synchronicity, though it had more to do with serendipity than design. But that same comfortable pattern was what gave me a sense midway through December that something was off. I had done enough stakeouts in my career to trust the sense that a new element had been introduced, something extremely subtle but still capable of throwing the pattern; a feeling that despite the regular crowd of people, at least one individual was repeatedly pacing me but remaining hidden in plain sight.

Like any good investigator, I began to pay even closer attention to my surroundings; by the week of the Christmas holiday, I thought perhaps it was time to change my pattern slightly in the hope I could shake lose my anonymous companion and put a face to the shadow I was nearly convinced had been following me for weeks.

Choosing the Thursday before the long holiday weekend at random, I went left instead of right at the entrance to the running path behind the station and began to work my normal route backwards. I had a general sense of my timing when running in the *other* direction and within five minutes of my usual appearance made it to the spot where it always felt like I picked up my shadow. Slowing to a trot, I kept myself merged into the flow of people as I scanned the crowd.

Mark Freidman was ostensibly stretching his quads while leaning against the small restroom on that part of the pathway; he was cleverly using the way the building was angled to keep an eye on runners coming down the trail from a protected spot by the water fountain. He looked completely innocuous, but the odds that it was a coincidence he'd be there at the same time as me, given how it was widely known that he kept bankers hours at the station, were long. Slowing to a stop, I considered my next move; given the allegations of harassment he'd lodged against me, the two of us were forbidden from interacting with each other, on the job or off. Accosting him would damage my already tarnished reputation further, possibly beyond repair.

I opted for a bit of subterfuge, and turned in the other direction, trotting to a park bench a few yards from the restrooms. Sitting down, I slid my iPhone out of my tights and cocked my head as though I were listening to something on my earbuds; glancing sideways, I turned a little more to ensure I was looking away from Mark and then took a deep breath.

"Yes," I said, loudly but not *too* loudly. "That's right. Next Tuesday." I paused, as if I were waiting for a response. "Well, that's the schedule for the docket---yes, I know that," I continued, acting like I was arguing with someone. "But the District Attorney—well, if you think that's the best option, fine. I'll get it to you tomorrow," I added with disgust.

Tapping my phone as though I were ending the call, I stood, stretched slightly to work out a kink that didn't exist in my back, then turned to start my jog again. Glancing at the photo I'd managed to take while "stretching," I confirmed Mark had bitten on my bait before sliding the phone back into my tights. I wasn't entirely certain I liked the idea that my nemesis had escalated to stalking, but now that I knew, it told me something about where the two of us stood.

I just wished to God I knew what that was.

Afterword

I had never intended for Vasily Korsokovach to leap into his own book, let alone an independent series where he would be the focus of attention. Any author is likely to tell you characters can sometimes take off in directions that you don't expect, even after – or perhaps *despite* – carefully plotting out every last aspect of a story. While I'm not *exactly* a planner-planner, I was just as surprised as everyone else when Vasily walked out of Sean Colbeth's life at the end of *Blindsided*. As those final paragraphs were being written, I found myself intrigued, wondering what might have happened to Vas *beyond* that watershed moment. I understood *why* he had acted the way he did, but would life in California measure up to the fantasy I suspected he had created? And could he truly leave everything he loved behind in Windeport?

I realized pretty quickly I wanted to get to know Vasily better. *Outsider* (the second book in the *Sean Colbeth Investigates* series) was already in the works at that point and gave me a chance to test drive the idea; before I knew it, *Pariah* popped into being and a new series was born. (Clearly Vas is an excellent negotiator.)

Technically, this is the first book in my *Vasily Korsokovach Investigates* series; I've attempted to write the two series so they can each stand alone, but since Vasily and Sean appear to have an affinity for working together, their stories are ultimately intertwined. Unfortunately, I wrote my first three books out of what would be considered chronological order; should you wish to experience Vasily's *entire* arc (so far) in a more "proper" timeline, here is my recommended reading order:

1. *Blindsided*
2. *Pariah*
3. *Outsider*

As new titles arrive, I'll continue to update the chronological list on my website (https://chrisjansmann.com/books/) so be sure to bookmark it for future reference.

ACKNOWLEDGEMENTS

The village that has quietly supported me on this journey is like no other.

To a person, they have provided me with valuable feedback at key points in my writing process; then, after having been so generous initially, happily took another whack at the second and third drafts, all the while gently pushing me forward. There is no way I could have done this without their invaluable help, timely advice and forthright willingness to give me the pure, unvarnished trust about what I have crafted.

As I write this, I've penned six novels in the overall series and am about to embark on the seventh. I know for certain, the wise observations, suggestions and, I have to admit, corrections have made my stories even better. I cannot say *thank you* enough to these amazing people:

Charlotte, Tristan and Lisa, aka **the Writing (S)quad of Doom**: thank you for keeping me honest, consistent, and realistic, especially given how different a character Vasily is from Sean. Finding a *new* voice was a challenge, especially one for someone with such a different set of life experiences than my own. My ability to query about the darndest things – and getting amazing answers back – is a gift that I treasure immensely.

Kristin: your initial suggestions were *huge* and helped me to both shape and smooth out parts of the story that were not quite ready for prime time... and lead me to thinking about the next book in this series (that hadn't been part of my initial plan).

And finally, my wife, **Paula**: you're the only person *besides* me that has read every iteration of this manuscript. There are times when I think you know my characters better than I do, which allows you to gently – but firmly – get me back on track when Vas tries to get too ornery. Thank you for your quiet support, which has kept me grounded as I found my way to the core of this adventure. You are my muse and my biggest fan, and there is absolutely no way I could have done this without you. My love is yours, always and forever.

--C

May 27, 2021

About the Author

Born and raised in Maine, Chris has spent nearly three decades as an IT nerd, writing just about everything *other* than a novel in the process. That changed in early 2019 when he was advised to find a way to wind down from his day job; sifting through his options, he recalled a childhood ambition to become a writer and quickly found himself weaving an entirely new world from the comfort of his laptop. *Pariah* is his third book, part of a planned pair of series featuring Chief Sean Colbeth and Detective Vasily Korsokovach.

Despite his love for the Northeast, the author escaped the cold for Arizona, where he currently resides with his beautiful wife, two cats, and a Shar-Pei mix that insists on being walked regularly.

For all of the latest information, including hints about upcoming books in both series, please visit the author's website at

https://chrisjansmann.com

facebook.com/christopherjansmann

instagram.com/chrisjansmann

amazon.com/author/chrisjansmann

bookbub.com/authors/christopher-h-jansmann

goodreads.com/chrisjansmann

mastodon.coffee/@chrisjansmann

www.ingramcontent.com/pod-product-compliance
Lightning Source LLC
Chambersburg PA
CBHW020611310726
48979CB00008B/1436/J

* 9 7 8 1 9 6 0 9 1 4 2 7 9 *